Out for the Count

A Finch & Fischer Mystery

J. New

Out for the Count
A Finch & Fischer Mystery Book 6

Cover design: Elizabeth Mackay
Interior Formatting: Jesse Gordon

ONE

The night air was fresh and dry. The cold snapped at the tip of Penny's nose and cheeks and she could feel her face glowing under the star flecked, deep black winter sky.

She looked down at her little Jack Russell Terrier, Fischer, trotting beside her, his head upright facing the stiff breeze as he walked in step. His tail was upright, and he looked as happy as he always did, seemingly unaffected by the cold. Her mother, in a fit of madness as far as Penny was concerned, had knitted him four woollen booties for the occasion and she wondered briefly if she should have put them on. His feet must be cold, treading the flagstone pavements of Thistle Grange. But just as quickly, she dismissed the idea. Dogs in human clothing drove her mad. It was ridiculous. Winter dog coats to keep them warm or even shoes to protect their pads while doing canicross or similar she could understand, but tutus and bows and little dresses were unnatural and undignified. Not to mention upsetting for the dog. And in some cases dangerous.

J. New

She'd read articles where dogs had overheated to due to restrictive clothing while others had become sick due to allergies to the fibers. No, her boy was perfectly content looking and feeling as nature intended. He looked up at her as though understanding he was the source of her musing. Eyes bright and sparkling, his happy cute expression bearing no resemblance to the wolves from which he was descended.

"Are you okay, little man?"

He woofed in response, tail wagging and tongue lolling in his usual smile.

"Yes, you're fine," Penny said, bending to scratch his ears. "Better than fine, Fish Face. You're perfect."

Fischer took a couple of steps forward, eager to get to the party on Cobbler's Lane. They could hear the sounds of revelry already.

Halloween was an ancient tradition. Older than the castle standing guard over the market town of Winstoke. Older even than the Pig and Whistle pub in Penny's home village of Cherrytree Downs. The party in Cobbler's Lane in the village of Thistle Grange, while not as old, had certainly been an annual event since Penny had been a schoolgirl. One of her earliest memories at primary school was her class spending days making costumes and masks to wear to the event.

Even though she was definitely classed as middle-aged, Penny still looked forward to the party. Bobbing for apples was a big draw, although she no longer participated, leaving the fun to the children and the odd adult male a bit worse for drink who was usually egged on by a group of friends. But it was all in good fun. She always attended the ghost story performance by the local story teller though. The whole downs community from the surrounding villages gathered annually for spooky fun. It was one of the highlights of the year, and Penny wouldn't dream of missing it.

The bright lights spilling out from Cobbler's Lane were inviting, drawing Penny closer. It had been a bit reckless to walk from Cherrytree Downs, but the moon was full and the night bright. She'd walked due east from home, following every hillock and rill of the familiar landscape to the edge of Cringle Wood where she'd climbed over the old stile by the fishing lodge and onto the road. The final mile walk from Holts End to Thistle Grange was a short step for Penny and Fischer, who were well used to rambling over the countryside. But she'd started to have a creeping doubt about the wisdom of coming by foot, knowing she may have to do it all again on the way home. But the first glint of coloured lights dispelled her concerns. She was ready to join the party.

She knew she could always get a lift back from someone if she needed to. Or, failing that, there was always a taxi. But the local taxi driver, Trevor Smith, was always a bit too friendly for Penny's liking. The idea of personal space was an alien concept to Trevor. He always came too close, his breath pungent, and he liked to touch her arm or her elbow when he spoke to her. 'Call me Trev, sweetheart,' he would say whenever they met. But Penny made a point of calling him Trevor. No, she'd avoid Trevor if she could. Anyway, Fischer preferred to walk, even on a cold night such as this.

The joyful sounds of the party, inviting and exciting, drew her closer. Penny loved this time of year. As a child it had been about the party, the trick or treating, well mainly the treats if she was honest, she never took part in the tricks as there was always a bowl of sweets offered at every door she and Susie had knocked on. Now she was fascinated by the history and traditions of the event itself, stemming as it did from the pagan festival Samhain, which welcomed in the harvest and the ushering in of the dark half of the year. It was originally believed that the barriers between the physical world and the spirit thinned or broke down during Samhain, allowing interaction between inhabitants of the two.

During ancient times, hearth fires in the homes were left to burn out while the harvest was gathered. Once complete, the celebrants joined the Druid priests to light a community fire and at the end took home a flame from the bonfire to relight their hearths.

Penny smiled, thinking there was no chance she'd be able to take a flaming torch back across the hills and valleys home to relight her wood burner. No, she'd stick to firelighters and a match.

In previous years, she'd gone dressed as a ghost using a bed sheet. This year she was once again dressed in white in the form of a doctor's white coat, a stethoscope and black rubber gloves. Her makeup gave her a crazy look with dark eyes peering out from white face. Her hair, untameable at the best of times, had been back-combed to within an inch of its life and now stuck up in all directions thanks to the copious amounts of hairspray. Tonight she was Doctor Frankenstein. She looked down fondly at Fischer. The illusion of a bolt through his neck collar was subtle but enough to mark him out as her creation, Frankenstein's monster. Admittedly an adorable one and not in the least bit scary.

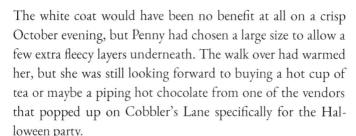

The white coat would have been no benefit at all on a crisp October evening, but Penny had chosen a large size to allow a few extra fleecy layers underneath. The walk over had warmed her, but she was still looking forward to buying a hot cup of tea or maybe a piping hot chocolate from one of the vendors that popped up on Cobbler's Lane specifically for the Halloween party.

Fischer trotted happily a couple of steps in front as they heard shrieks and squeals of delight and terror from a group of schoolchildren who came running from behind a row of shops. They were being pursued by a demon from the amateur dramatic society. It was the patron and director herself, former television actress Chase Scarlett, dressed in a long tight black dress, black wig and scarily green make-up. She was clearly the matriarch of a fiendish family. She greeted Penny with a devilish cackle and raised her arms above her head, long blood red fingernails glinting in the light as she cast a spell on Penny.

"Ha ha Doctor Frankenstein at last," Chase said in her deep resonant actor's voice. "Prepare to meet your doom." She lowered her arms and smiled, revealing a row of realistically pointed teeth. "Or maybe just a hot chocolate and a bit of fun?"

Penny laughed. "If it's a choice, I'll go with the chocolate and fun thanks, Chase."

The children came running back and crowded around the actress, taking her by the hand and dragging her back to continue the quest.

"My audience awaits, Penny. Enjoy yourself."

The rest of the theatre group were taking it in turns to lead small groups of children on the scary Halloween walk behind Cobbler's Lane where luminous ghosts, skeletons and live actors jumped out to frighten them. All manner of devilish trickery was arrayed in the dark for their terror and delight, according to the advertising posters Penny had seen everywhere during the last week. It was like a ghost train but walking instead of riding.

Penny and Fischer continued their walk, heading towards the Pot and Kettle, her favourite cafe in the village. It was usually closed at this time of night, but always opened for special events. The windows were decorated with cobwebs and silhouettes of witches on broomsticks, their black familiars staring out with glowing orange eyes.

Suddenly, someone reached out and grabbed Penny by the shoulder. "Got you!" said a spooky voice. She gave out a scream of surprise and Fischer barked once before whining and wiggling his bottom in recognition. Penny turned and saw Mr Kelly. His expression changed to one of shock. Then he laughed.

"Penny. Gosh, I am sorry. I thought you were Laura. She's dressed up as a mad scientist too."

Penny laughed. "Hello, Mr Kelly." He was dressed as Lurch from the Adams Family. It was a very good likeness.

"She was just here a minute ago." He glanced around, looking for his daughter, but she was impossible to spot among the crowd.

"I dare say there will be plenty of mistaken identities tonight, considering there are so many similar costumes. I hope you find her."

"I'm sure I will," he said, bending to give Fischer an ear scratch. "The least scary monster here tonight. Oh, there's Laura now. Sorry again, Penny. See you soon."

Penny waved to Laura and watched as her father explained what he'd done, causing her to laugh raucously.

"Penny Finch."

She turned and saw a pair of zombies ambling towards her, arms outstretched, hands limp at the wrists and heads cocked to one side as they moaned and shuffled in her direction. They looked like they were auditioning for a remake of Sean of the Dead, one of her favourite comedy spoof films. She wasn't a particular film buff, preferring books, but Susie had insisted on watching it one night and she'd thoroughly enjoyed it.

Even under heavy make-up and beneath tattered rags, Penny instantly knew this was Susie, and shuffling along at her side was her new boyfriend, the young and handsome newspaper photographer, Tom. He had a camera slung round his neck and was breaking character every few moments to snap a photo.

Penny walked closer, smiling and admiring her brilliant costume. Susie placed her hands on Penny's shoulders, moaning and rolling her eyes as she leaned forward, pretending to bite her neck. Fischer barked in confusion. This was Susie, a friend, but she appeared to be attacking Penny. However, his concern disappeared when Penny laughed.

"Yep, okay, you got me. I'm a zombie Frankenstein now."

"Would Frankenstein's monster become a zombie if he was bitten?" Tom said, pretending to muse seriously over a philosophical question. "Surely he's already a zombie of sorts. What if a vampire bit a zombie? Would it then turn into something different altogether? Or what if a werewolf was bitten by a zombie? Would it turn back into a normal person the next day and become a zombie werewolf during a full moon?"

Penny and Susie laughed dutifully at the attempted joke, but when Tom carried on in the same vein for another minute, the humour was wearing thin. Penny felt her smile slipping and she could see Susie's eyes glazing over.

Susie thumped his shoulder playfully. "I think we get the message." Tom put his arm around her shoulder.

"Is it okay for zombies to have hot chocolate?" Penny asked.

"Just as long as there's a shot of rum in it, I can drink any-thing," Tom said with a grin.

Susie removed herself from under his arm. "I thought you were driving later?"

Tom shrugged and pulled a wry face. "Yeah, I am. Maybe we can have a few beers or a bottle of wine when we get back to your place?" He reached for her hand.

"I'll have chocolate for now.

Penny took out her purse and handed Tom a ten-pound note. "Maybe you could go over to the Pot and Kettle and get us three hot chocolates. Without the rum," she added.

Tom took the note. "Happy to help." He turned and zombie walked away moaning hot chocolate in a zombie voice. He turned back briefly and grinned at them both, waiting for a laugh. They obliged.

"Did you just send my boyfriend to the shop?" Susie said, hooking her arm through Penny's.

Penny didn't reply. She thought Susie seemed happy, but

there was something else below the surface she couldn't put a name to. "It's nice to see you having some fun, Susie. I thought the children would be here, though. Where are they?"

Susie took a couple of steps before replying. "They're with James, and her, for a holiday," she said, with a slightly bitter emphasis on 'her.'

Even though it had been some time ago, and although her friend was in the throes of an exciting new relationship, it was clear to Penny that Susie was still bitter and saddened by the breakup of her marriage.

"Has James taken them out of school for a holiday?"

Susie shook her head. "No, it's half term."

"Half term isn't this week, is it?"

"The headmaster moved it so it could fit in with the building work. The old heating system needed urgent repair. I bet they're still the same radiators that were there when old Fred was in school."

"The kids are probably having a good time, Susie. And it means you can let your hair down for once without worrying about them."

"I know. I just wanted them to come here. How many years did we come to the Halloween party when we were kids? I don't think I missed a single year since I learned to walk."

"I only missed that one year when I cut up my mother's best bed sheet for a ghost outfit," Penny said.

Susie laughed. "I'd forgotten that. Has she forgiven you yet?"

"Well, I'm here, aren't I?"

The two friends laughed and continued on into the crowd.

———— ● ————

Suddenly, a roar went up from one end of Cobbler's Lane and a group of men dressed as St. Trinians' schoolgirls appeared. They cheered and let off party poppers. Blowing hard on whistles to scare away the demons, but unfortunately they also scared a few of the younger children as well. It took a few friendly but stern words from Chase Scarlett to calm to them down. Penny looked down at Fischer in concern, but he was taking it all in his stride, thankfully. More interested and alert than afraid.

The St. Trinians' group was actually the Winstoke cricket team, their behaviour encouraged by team captain Harry Slade. He was a big man with hairy, muscular shoulders sticking out from his dress. He was also wielding a cricket bat. Slade was not known for his subtle nip and tuck play of a first class batsman. His strokes were wild, heavy haymakers, but when they connected with the ball, he sent it flying into the boundary every time. Any half decent bowler could take his stumps after bowling a few good overs, but a few overs were all Harry needed to notch up the sixes needed to give his side a handy haul of runs early in any innings. In the local league, Harry Slade was a star and a legend, and he knew it.

The shoes he wore were ladies with chunky heels. Penny had no idea where he could have found a large enough size to fit him, but was sure they would break under his hairy tree-trunk legs. She shared a glance with Susie, both of them shaking their heads in a mix of amusement and despair. There was something about sportsmen and their desire to dress as ladies on a night out. The cricket team was notorious for it.

Filling the Pig and Whistle in Cherrytree Downs after a match or a fancy dress birthday party for one of the team members.

Old Fred, the wicketkeeper and the announcer at all the village events, didn't look as enthusiastic as the younger members, though. He was now the longest serving member and was outnumbered by a fresh batch of players. He was wearing a St Trinians' uniform but had on a sensible pair of brogues with thick socks, and in deference to his age had been allowed to wear a woolly hat and his parka to stave off the cold.

The team strutted past Penny and Susie, who were standing on the pavement of the narrow alley watching the parade of ghouls and goblins. Harry Slade doffed his straw hat as he approached them.

"Ladies," he said with a wink. He stepped forward, looking for all the world as if he was going to kiss Penny. She recoiled and Fischer jumped up, his paws on Slade's knees. The man took a step back as the little dog's claws snagged his tights.

"Hey, watch your dog there, Penny," Slade said. "He's going to ladder my tights."

Just as Penny pulled Fischer back, he'd only jumped up to say hello, Slade saw someone in the crowd and shouted out unpleasantly.

"Hey you, Martin, you blood swine. I want a word with you."

"Language, Slade," Susie said. "There are children here."

But Slade wasn't listening. He walked up to Martin, the local garage mechanic and a good friend of Penny's, grabbed him by the shoulder and spun him round.

Martin was wearing an exceptionally well put together

vampire costume, dressed as a classic Victorian character in a white ruffled shirt beneath a tapestry waistcoat and a long black coat. Black breeches and high boots, a cane and a top hat finished the costume off perfectly. His make up was ghostly white with blood-red lips and dark eyes. Penny was incredibly impressed. Harry Slade looked like a massive hairy troll next to the mild-mannered mechanic.

"What do you think you're playing at, you bloody cretin?" Slade spat in Martin's face. "All you needed to do was declare the team bus fit for service. There's nothing wrong with it. I should know. I drive the damn thing. How are we supposed to get the team halfway across the country for our promotion play off match if we don't have a bus to go in? You're going to mess everything up, you moron. You better write up a new certificate. I'll be in your garage first thing in the morning to collect the paperwork."

As small as Martin was next to the cricket captain, he showed no signs of being intimidated.

"The bus is unsafe," Martin replied calmly. "I told you to bring it in for a service in the summer. It's an old bus and needs more than just a new oil filter like you said it did. It needs a lot of work. As it is at the moment, it's not fit for the road. You'd be endangering the lives of every passenger on board, not to mention other road users and pedestrians. I don't have time now to fix it before your promotion match, Harry, I have other customer's vehicles to attend to. I gave you plenty of notice, so I'd have the time I need to get it back up to standard. There's no point crying now you've left it too late."

Harry raised the cricket bat and for one awful moment, Penny thought he was going to hit Martin with it. But he just shoved it into Martin's shoulder. "You better be at the garage tomorrow with the paperwork or you'll be the one in tears."

Martin staggered backwards. "There's nothing I can do, Harry."

"You'll be sorry," Harry said, shoving him again.

Penny was just about to go over to try and calm things down when a man dressed as The Phantom of the Opera stepped up. He spoke authoritatively from behind his half mask.

"Harry Slade. Calm down and control yourself or I'll be asking you to leave."

Slade spun round, fury in his eyes. "Says who?"

The instant fury drained from his face as the phantom removed his mask to reveal the handsome features of Detective Inspector John Monroe.

"Fine," Harry said, storming off. But not before he'd given Martin a last venomous look.

Fischer on hearing John's voice began whining and straining at the lead, desperate to get to his friend. Penny let him go and Fischer bounded up, bottom wiggling in ecstasy as he jumped up at the detective. John scooped him up and valiantly ignoring the little dog giving his ears a thorough wash, walked over to Penny.

Penny was very pleased to see him, almost as much as Fischer was.

"Hello John, come on, Fischer, get down now."

"Hi, Penny, hi, Susie. I thought I'd find you here somewhere. Nice hair do," he added, peering at Penny's head with a raised eyebrow.

"Thank you. I like to make the effort when I go out. Hopefully, I won't find it left on the pillow when I get up in the morning. I thought you were working?"

"I am actually." He indicated a couple of constables outside a pop-up shop talking to a group of children. "It's part of the police community outreach program. Warning children about stranger danger. It's safe for the kids at an organised event like this as they are accompanied by their parents or an adult family member. But running around on their own, in disguises, trick or treating and knocking on the doors of strangers can put them in unnecessary danger."

"Ellen and Billy are going trick or treating with their father," Susie said. "Seems like it's something we imported from America, but they're really looking forward to it."

"Actually, I believe it's the other way around," Penny said. "It was the Celts that started it over two thousand years ago with their festival of Samhain, and they lived in what is now Ireland, the UK and Northern France."

"And there speaks the librarian," John said, gazing fondly at Penny. "I seem to remember carving turnips when we were young, rather than pumpkins."

"Known as Jack-o'-lanterns," Penny said. "That's also an interesting story, but I'll tell you another time."

"No, go on," Susie said. "You've piqued my interest."

"Okay, if you're sure?"

"Of course I am. I like your stories, Penny. Besides, we need to wait for Tom to get back, anyway. Go on, what about the lanterns?"

"Well, according to the story a man named Stingy Jack invited the Devil to have a drink with him, but as his name suggests, he didn't want to pay for it, so he convinced the Devil to turn himself into a coin that Jack used to buy their drinks. Once he'd done so, Jack decided to keep the money and put it in his pocket next to a silver cross, which prevented the Devil from changing back into his original form. Jack eventually freed the Devil but under the condition he wouldn't bother Jack for one year, and if he should die the Devil wouldn't claim his soul. The following year, Jack again tricked the Devil into climbing a tree to pick a piece of fruit. While he was up there, Jack carved the sign of the cross into the bark of the tree so the Devil couldn't come down until he'd promised Jack he wouldn't bother him for ten more years. Soon after, Jack died. The legend has it that God wouldn't let such an unsavory figure into heaven. The Devil, upset by the tricks Jack had played on him and keeping his word not to claim his soul, wouldn't let Jack into hell. Instead, he sent Jack off into the dark with only a burning coal to light his way. Jack put the coal into a carved-out turnip and has been roaming the earth ever since. The Irish began to refer to this ghostly figure as 'Jack of the Lantern,' and then it simply became 'Jack-o'-lantern.' The end." She took a bow.

"Oh my goodness, Penny, I've got goosebumps," Susie said, shivering.

"That's a great story for Halloween," John said. "You should be the story teller, you know."

Penny smiled and shook her head. "There's already an excellent story teller."

Tom reappeared, balancing three paper cups of hot chocolate. He gave Penny and Susie theirs, then looked slightly embarrassed at John. "Sorry, Inspector, I didn't get you one."

"No need, Tom, I'm on duty. And I'd better get back to it." He bent and gave Penny a kiss on the cheek. "I'll catch up with you later. By all."

Penny watched him slip back into the crowd, looking exceptionally handsome in his Victorian Gentleman's opera tuxedo and her heart skipped a beat. Then the moment was ruined by the appearance of Trevor Smith at her shoulder.

TWO

Trevor took a gulp from a small pop bottle, a child's drink with the label torn off. It was obvious to Penny that whatever the bottle had once contained, it was now filled with alcohol. The glue that once held the sticker was covered in grime and pocket fluff. He drew his lips over his teeth and let out a satisfied sigh. His warm fetid breath rolling over Penny's face in waves. She turned away in revulsion.

"All right, sweetheart," he asked her, taking another sip from the bottle before screwing on the cap and slipping into his jacket pocket.

"What have you come as?" Susie asked, looking him up and down. "A tramp?"

Trevor laughed sarcastically. "I see you came as yourself, Susie."

Susie rolled her eyes, but felt Tom stiffen beside her.

"I'm not here to muck about drinking hot chocolate,"

Trevor said. "Some of us have to work for a living. I'm looking to see if anyone wants a taxi back to town or the villages."

Tom stepped between Susie and Penny and gave Trevor a flinty look.

"Why don't you shove off, Pal," he told the older man.

Trevor laughed, but there was no humor in it. There was a nasty gleam in his eye. "Isn't it past your bedtime, kid? No offence, but I'm more afraid of Penny's dog than you."

"Come on, Trevor," Susie said in a conciliatory and friendly manner. "We're supposed to be having fun tonight."

"You and me can have a bit of fun on our own later if you like, Pen," Trevor said, sidling closer. "I won't charge you for a ride. We can come to some sort of arrangement."

Penny was just about to tell Trevor exactly what he could do with his arrangements when Fischer growled. It was low and very menacing. The little dog took a step toward the taxi driver, hackles raised and sharp teeth bared. Tom took a step back and Trevor grinned, although he too moved away from Fischer. He gave Penny a last glance and, pulling the now familiar bottle from his pocket, took a swig and walked away.

"What a creep," Susie said, disgust written widely on her face. "Was he drinking?"

"I don't think it was cherryade in his bottle, Susie," Penny said. "Maybe I should ask John if he can spare an officer to take him home. He shouldn't be driving on his own, let-alone with passengers."

They heard Trevor's voice rise again. He was shouting at Martin, the mechanic.

"Martin's getting all the nutters tonight, isn't he?" Tom said. "I saw what happened with that bloke Slade before."

"Hey you. Martin," Trevor hollered. "You did a shoddy job on my taxi, mate. I had a passenger in the car when it went off the road. All thanks to your poor workmanship. If you hadn't done such a bad job, I wouldn't have ended up in Tomkin's field. The young lad I was carrying sprained his wrist and got a bloody nose, thanks to you. He's talking about suing and if he does, you're gonna pay for it. Understood?"

Trevor was jabbing his finger in Martin's face, while the other hand swung the pop bottle about.

"Your taxi was in perfect condition when it left my garage, Trevor. I've told you before if you don't like my work you can go elsewhere. In fact, don't bring your vehicle in again. I neither need nor want your business."

"Fine, but I'm bringing you the bill for the garage that'll make good your bad work. I expect you to pay it."

"You'll be waiting a long time, Trevor. And as far as blame goes, I think you need to look a bit closer to home." He pointed at the bottle in Trevor's hand. "You need to stop or you'll lose your license. You're endangering yourself, your passengers and other road users. Give it up before you get locked up."

"Don't you threaten me."

"It's not a threat, Trevor," Martin said with tremendous calm. "It's friendly advice. Clean yourself up or I'll go to the police. If you carry on like you are, you'll do far more harm than giving someone a bloody nose or denting Tomkin's hedge."

"Wow, it's all happening in Cobbler's Lane tonight," Tom said, scrunching up his paper cup and throwing it in the nearest bin. "Now it looks as though another Count Dracula's about to get involved. Maybe he'll turn them into bats."

Penny and Susie turned to see Gary Tate in full Dracula

costume step out of the old furniture shop. His outfit was re-markably similar to Martin's Penny thought. They must have hired them from the same fancy dress shop. There was a Thatchings logo hung over the doorway. He had obviously hired the venue for the night to promote his business. Gary was serving a sample menu from his bed and breakfast, which was open in the weekday evenings as a restaurant. As well as drumming up trade for the B and B itself.

He moved forward, inserting himself between the two ar-guing men. It was not like Gary Tait to put himself in danger. Penny knew him from school and he had always been a shy, awkward boy who grew to be a quiet and kind man. Unfortu-nately, he had married the local harridan and was also a much hen-pecked and bullied husband. Gary hated confrontation of any sort and Penny could see now he was ill at ease with this show of bravado.

"Guys, can you sort this out without shouting? There are families with children trying to enjoy their evening. They don't need to see you both yelling at each other. Perhaps you could discuss the problem quietly somewhere else?"

Gary was standing between the mechanic and the taxi driver, although his concentration was on Trevor as he was the real troublemaker. He was no smaller than either of them, but given his skinny frame, he looked as though he'd keel over if they both sneezed at the same time. Penny found herself really proud of Gary. He was obviously nervous but stood his ground, getting his message across politely but firmly. Then Cheryl Tate screeched from inside the furniture shop.

"Stop being so soft, Gary. Tell them to clear off. It's bad for trade."

Even from where she was stood, Penny could see Gary's shoulders stiffen and his jaw clench. He looked at the two men, imploring them to move on.

Trevor walked off, deliberately barging into Martin's shoulder as he went past. Martin nodded to Gary and moved in the opposite direction. Penny gave him a sympathetic look and mouthed, 'Are you okay?' Martin nodded, but he looked nervous. Trevor Smith was a rude, coarse man and not well liked, but Penny had never thought he was dangerous. Maybe Martin knew differently. Or perhaps he was thinking about the altercation with Harry Slade?

Gary was now handing out sweets to a group of children. Telling silly jokes and making them laugh. It was a shame he didn't have children of his own, Penny thought. He was really good with kids.

"Gary," Cheryl shrieked again. "Stop talking to every waif and stray and get back here and help me. Do I have to do everything myself? I swear this business would collapse if it wasn't for me. You're useless."

Susie looked at Penny with a mixture of shock, sympathy, and embarrassment on Gary's behalf.

"God, Penny, she is awful. I don't know how Gary puts up with it."

But Penny wasn't listening, she was watching Gary. Something had changed. He took a step towards the open door and was bathed in light from the shop. He straightened his shoulders and lifted his head. He appeared to grow taller. Bulk out. It was like looking at a different person. Then he spoke.

"Cheryl," his voice was strong but his tone mild. "I've had enough. Every moment of happiness I've ever had you've ruined. I'm unhappy and I'm tired of being unhappy. This marriage has been nothing but misery for both of us. Cheryl, I'm leaving you. I want a divorce."

The crowd surrounding them was so quiet you could have heard a pin drop. Penny's breath was momentarily snatched away at Gary's announcement, but seconds later, she felt euphoric. Inside, she was cheering and clapping and willing Gary on. With one last look at his stunned wife, Gary turned on his heel and disappeared at the end of the lane. Enveloped in darkness.

"Wow," Susie said. "That was brilliant. I never thought Gary Tait would muster the courage to finally leave Cheryl. Good on him."

"He was really brave," Penny said. "I hope he sticks to his guns. He deserves a much better life than the one he's had with her."

Tom was grinning broadly at Susie. "You were right, babe. This is brilliant fun. Better than the TV. I thought watching a bunch of country bumpkins with sheets over their heads would be boring, but this is the best Halloween I can ever remember. What do you guys do for bonfire night?" he laughed. "You know, my mates told me I was mad for taking a job on a little local newspaper that distributes to a few cottages and a couple of sheep rather than one in the city. I bet they're not having half as much fun. I wouldn't miss this for the world."

Penny turned away so Susie wouldn't see her look of revulsion. Martin and Gary were friends of hers, not sources of amusement. She was beginning to wonder what Susie saw in Tom. He was young and good looking, yes, but he was also immature and, quite frankly, a bit silly. She took a deep breath and turned back, pasting a bright smile on her face. A quick glance at Susie and it was apparent she was feeling the same way. Even beneath her zombie make-up, Penny could see her blushing.

"Is this a friend of yours, Penny?" Tom asked, indicating a man making an obvious beeline for their group, and Penny in particular. Penny shook her head. She knew it was Richard Sole, a recent newcomer, but she'd never spoken to him. He was eating from a large bag of sweets and naturally was surrounded immediately by a group of young children dressed as pixies and goblins. "Get your own," he snarled.

The group of kids looked hurt until Chase Scarlett gathered them up and bought a large bucket of confectionery for them to share, and entertained them with an improvised performance of the wicked witch from The Wizard of Oz.

"You're from my village, aren't you?" Sole said to Penny.

Penny thought it more than a bit presumptuous referring to Cherrytree Downs as *his* village. He'd only lived there a month or two at most. He'd bought and moved into the large detached cottage, a well known listed building surrounded by high hedges with a wide gravel drive. It was topped off with an ornate thatched roof. He'd also bought the land next to it and was already expanding his new home by building a massive garage for his small but increasing fleet of fancy sports cars. There seemed to be a new one appearing daily. Richard Sole was a lottery winner. The rumour was he'd won a jackpot of around two million pounds. Although depending on who you talked to, the figure increased by another million each time. But, however much he'd won, it was obviously substantial.

"Yes, I live in Cherrytree Downs," Penny said now. "I've lived there all my life, actually."

"I do too," Susie said, but Richard hardly gave her a glance.

"So, what do you think of the garage?"

"The garage?" Penny said. "The one you're building?"

"No, not mine," he answered impatiently. "I mean the eyesore that belongs to that mechanic, Martin. It's a disgrace. It totally ruins the look of my place as it's next door. It should be torn down. I've made him an offer he can't refuse. As soon as he clears off out of my village, I'll pull it down. I've got plans to build a games room with a snooker table, pinball machine and some of those old space invader machines. I've already put feelers out through various dealers to get the ones I used to play on when I was at school. Money's no object and I want the best. I thought I'd get one of those big video games from the arcades as well. The ones built like a car or a motorbike that you pretend to drive."

"Don't you have enough cars already?" Susie said bluntly. She was peeved at being rudely ignored. "You can only drive one at a time."

"Never," Sole barked out with a strident laugh. "I'm rich. I can have as many as I like."

"Personally, I think Martin takes very good care of his garage," Penny said. "It's always neat and tidy. I don't think it's an eyesore at all and he provides a vital service for the villagers. Myself included."

"Well, I won't take my cars there. He might be able to patch up an old banger, but I wouldn't let him work on any of my classics. I'll get him out, you'll see. I want my games room." He was staring down Cobbler's Lane, watching Martin walk away into the darkness. "Not much of a party this, is it? Here you are, kid," he said, thrusting the bag of sweets into Tom's gut. "I've had enough of this rubbish. I'm off."

The three of them stared after him as he approached a red sports car that had been inconsiderately abandoned at the end of the lane.

"What an insufferable oaf," Susie said. "He obviously came over just to show off about his wealth."

"That's the second time I've been called a kid," Tom said sulkily. "And what do I want with a bag of sweets?"

Susie took them and walked over to give them to Chase Scarlett. She returned a moment later.

"So, what should we do now?"

"Actually, I think I've had enough, Susie. I'm ready to head home."

"Do you need a lift, Penny?" It was John who'd suddenly materialised at her shoulder. Fischer was going frantic, trying to climb up his leg. "I'll need to go into Winstoke and debrief the team, but I can drop you off first if you like?"

Penny nodded. She liked the thought of going home with John. "Yes, please. That would be great."

"Sir, can I have a word?"

It was one of the constables she had seen earlier. John walked away to discuss whatever it was in private, but returned a couple of minutes later. "Sorry, Penny, I'll need to be here for another half hour or so. Can you wait?"

"We can take her," Susie said. "Tom's parked just up the

road and we're going to Cherrytree Downs, anyway. Is that all right with you, Penny?"

"I'll go with Susie and Tom now, John. But if you're back in time, perhaps we could pop over to the Pig and Whistle for a nightcap?

Monroe nodded. "A great idea. I'll call for you when I'm finished."

A sudden roar of a powerful engine shattered the air as Richard Sole's car took off, wheels spinning and exhaust blasting smoke. Monroe watched it thoughtfully.

"I'll need to keep an eye on him," he said, more to himself than anyone else.

Tom's car was a small grey hatchback of indeterminate age. It might have actually been white at some point in its past, but now was covered with a layer of grime and dirt. The back seat was littered with all kinds of newspapers, empty shopping bags, and an open packet of chocolate biscuits, which Penny put on the parcel shelf behind her so as not to tempt Fischer. There were a couple of discarded pop cans in the foot well which she discovered only after she'd crushed one underfoot getting in.

"Just shove it all out of the way, Penny," Tom said cheerfully. "Chuck it on the floor. It's fine. I'll clear it up later."

Penny gathered everything up and put it on the floor behind the passenger seat. Judging from the dates on the newspapers, this stuff had been sitting in the back of the car for weeks, if not months. After she settled Fischer next to her, he gave her a look. Penny agreed with him. She didn't believe Tom would be tidying his car anytime soon, either.

After a few minutes of careful driving, maneuvering around families who were walking back home through the village, they came out onto the dark country road. But they hadn't gone far when Tom braked and pulled over. Parking at the side of the road. He'd spotted the church.

"Graveyard," he said excitedly. "Come on, it is Halloween. Let's run through the cemetery for a laugh."

Penny was aghast. They weren't children, they were grown adults. All she wanted to do was go home and have a quiet drink in the pub with John, or failing that curl up with a good book and a cup of tea. She frowned. She sounded boring even to herself. She'd found recently that while hanging out with Tom made Susie feel young, it had the opposite effect on her. She always felt old in his company. But she could see Susie really wanted to go. She'd turned back looking at Penny, a half uncertain half pleading look on her face. It was obvious she wanted to spend time with Tom, even though Penny secretly thought she was pandering to him unnecessarily. But she didn't want to spoil her friend's fun.

Penny nodded. "Yes, all right, why not? Halloween only comes once a year." Thank goodness, she added to herself.

The cemetery, even on a night as lively as Halloween, was quiet. The distant sounds of the village celebrations were muffled, replaced by the soft rustling of autumn leaves and the occasional hoot of an owl. The tall, ancient trees that bordered the graveyard cast long, haunting shadows on the ground, their branches swaying gently in the night breeze.

Fischer, sensing the change in atmosphere, moved cautiously. His ears were perked up, and every so often, he'd stop to sniff the air or investigate a particularly intriguing scent on the ground. Penny watched him, appreciating his instincts and wondering what stories the cemetery held for him. She'd never walked him around here before.

Tom, with his youthful energy, seemed eager to explore. He pulled Susie along, their shared laughter a stark contrast to the solemnity of their surroundings. Penny watched them for a moment, noting how their figures became smaller as they ventured deeper into the graveyard.

Choosing to explore a different part of the cemetery, Penny walked along the old stone wall, her fingers occasionally brushing against the cold, rough surface. The gravestones, each unique in design and inscription, stood as silent reminders of the village inhabitants who'd passed away. Some were recent, with fresh flowers laid at their base, while others were old and worn, their inscriptions faded by time.

It was Fischer's sudden change in behavior that alerted Penny to something amiss. He began to whine, then bark furiously, pulling on his lead with an urgency she'd rarely seen before. Penny followed his lead, her heart rate quickening with a mix of curiosity and apprehension.

As they approached a particularly old gravestone, the full moon emerged from behind a cloud, casting a pale light on the scene before her. It was a body, lying still on the ground. Penny's breath caught in her throat as she recognized the face: Martin, the village mechanic.

Shock and disbelief washed over Penny. She knelt beside him, checking for a pulse she knew she wouldn't find, her mind racing. Martin had been more than just the village mechanic to her; he had been a friend, someone she had shared countless conversations and memories with.

Fischer, sensing Penny's distress, stayed close, his whining growing more pronounced. Penny hugged him, drawing some comfort from his presence.

The sound of hurried footsteps broke the heavy silence. Susie and Tom approached, their faces under the zombie makeup even more pale in the moonlight.

"Penny, what's happened? Why did Fischer bark like that?" Susie's voice was filled with concern.

Penny struggled to find her voice, the weight of the discovery pressing down on her. "It's Martin," she finally whispered. "He's dead."

Susie's eyes widened in shock, and she knelt beside Penny, her hand covering her mouth. Tom, not having known Martin, looked on with a mix of confusion and concern.

The reality of the situation began to sink in. They were in a cemetery on Halloween night, with the lifeless body of a friend. The implications were chilling.

Penny knew she had to call John. She reached for her phone, her fingers shaking. Her mind racing with questions: How had Martin ended up here? What had happened to him? And most importantly, who could have done this?

The night, which had begun with playful exploration and laughter, had taken a dark and tragic turn.

THREE

The chilling discovery of Martin's body had cast a heavy pall over the cemetery. The once silent and serene atmosphere was now thick with tension and grief. Penny's heart raced, her emotions a whirlwind of shock, sorrow, and anger. The weight of the situation pressed down on her, making the air feel thick and oppressive.

The distant sounds of Halloween festivities seemed worlds away, replaced by the haunting silence of the graveyard. Every rustle of leaves, every flapping of the raven's wings and the caws of the jackdaws seemed amplified, adding to the eerie atmosphere.

Suddenly, the stillness was shattered by a bright flash of light. Penny's instincts kicked in, and she spun around, her eyes narrowing as they landed on Tom, camera in hand. The audacity of his actions, given the gravity of the situation, was like a slap in the face.

"What do you think you're doing?" Penny's voice was sharp, her anger evident. She took a step toward Tom, her hands clenched into fists.

Tom, taken aback by Penny's reaction, tried to defend himself. "Look, I'm sorry, but I'm a photographer. This could be my first major story. It's my job."

Penny's eyes blazed with fury. "Martin was more than just a headline to me. He was my friend! How dare you treat this like some sensational scoop?"

Tom looked genuinely conflicted, torn between his professional instincts and the gravity of the situation. "I didn't mean to be insensitive. I just... I've never been in a situation like this before."

Before the situation could escalate further, Susie stepped in, her voice calm but firm. "Tom," she said, placing a gentle hand on his arm, "Penny's right. We've both known Martin for years. This isn't just a story for us. It's personal."

She turned to face Tom fully, her gaze unwavering. "Give me the camera. I promise I'll talk to John Monroe. We'll handle this story with the respect it deserves. Your photos will be used, but not like this. Not now."

Tom hesitated for a moment, then, with a resigned sigh, handed over his camera. The gravity of the situation appeared to finally dawn on him.

Penny, still seething, turned away. She needed a moment to collect herself, to process everything. But as she did, something caught her eye. She'd seen it on the periphery in the brief light, but only now recognised it for what it was. A clue. The flash from Tom's camera had illuminated markings on the ground behind Martin. A trail of disturbed grass and earth that led back to the road. It was clear evidence that Martin's body had been moved.

Her investigative instincts kicked in. She reached for her phone, dialing John's number.

His voice, warm and familiar, came through the line. "Penny, sorry, I might be a bit later than planned, but hopefully still in time for that nightcap."

Penny took a deep breath, trying to steady herself. "John, something's happened. I'm in the graveyard just outside of Thistle Grange. It's Martin. I think... I think he's been murdered."

"Are you all right, Penny?"

Penny was suddenly very grateful to hear his voice. John's first concern was always for her.

"I'm all right. It's a shock. Martin was my friend. Who would do something like this?"

"I'll be there as soon as I can, Penny," Monroe said gently. "I'm leaving now."

She could hear him moving purposefully through the crowds at the party as he spoke to her. "Are you on your own?"

"No, Susie and Tom are here. We'll move away and wait for you nearer the gate."

"I'll see you in a short while. Hang in there. I won't be long."

Penny hung up and turned to her companions. "We need to move away so we don't contaminate the scene. I've told John we'll meet him nearer the gate."

Susie came over and gave a hug. "I'm so sorry, Penny. I can't believe anyone would want to hurt Martin. John will find out who's responsible."

"Thanks, Susie."

Penny called Fischer, and he trotted by her side while Susie and Tom strode ahead, arms around one another, heads bent in quiet conversation. Penny used the torch function on her phone to scan the ground. As well as the drag marks leading back to the road, she could also see indents left by the heels of what looked like ladies' shoes. Not a fine stiletto, but they'd sunk slightly into the soft earth, leaving a definite trail. Having hiked over from home, Penny was wearing her walking boots. Susie was wearing a pair of heeled shoes. Tom was wearing trainers. But none of them had walked on this area.

They'd only just reached the gate to the churchyard when flashing blue lights appeared and a police vehicle parked up. Immediately behind Penny recognised John's car, and behind that a white van, no doubt containing the crime scene technicians. As John alighted, she could see he was still in his Halloween costume, but without the mask. He'd also removed his tie. He bounded over to her, concern marring his handsome features.

"Are you okay?" He asked, taking her by the shoulders. She nodded. "I'm very sorry about Martin, Penny. I know he was a friend of yours. I didn't know him well, but he was a good man. Believe me when I say I'll move heaven and earth to find out what happened to him and punish those responsible."

"Thank you, John."

"What were you doing in the graveyard? I thought you were going straight home?"

"Believe me, it wasn't my idea. Tom thought it would be fun to wander around the graveyard on Halloween. And as he was our driver, I could hardly say no."

"Oh, I see," he said, glancing back to where Tom and Susie were being interviewed by two constables.

"There's one other thing. Tom is the photographer with the paper and had his camera with him for the party. He's taken a photograph of Martin. I got angry with him and Susie took the camera."

"Damn fool. Wait here, I'll get it bagged up and taken to the station." He was back a moment later. "Do you feel up to giving me your statement?" he asked, as technicians decked in white coveralls made their way to the scene. They looked like ghosts, Penny thought. It sent a shiver running down her spine.

"Yes, that's fine."

"Okay. We can sit in my car where there's light. But first I need to look at the scene. Here, take the car keys and get warm. I won't be long."

"Penny," Susie called to her as she walked to the exit. "Are you ready to go?"

"Not yet. I need to give my statement. Have you two finished?"

"Yes. Do you want us to wait?"

"No, it's fine, Susie, honestly. John will take me home. You two go, there's no point you hanging around."

"If you're sure?"

"I am, Susie. You and Tom go home. I'll be fine. Goodnight, Tom."

"Night, Penny. And er, sorry about earlier. You know, with the camera."

Penny gave a brief smile and nodded. Putting him out of his misery. He was looking at the ground, hands deep in his pockets and shuffling his feet. He was obviously acutely embarrassed. "Thank you, Tom."

Penny settled into the passenger seat of John's car with Fischer curled up on her lap. She was awoken moments later by the driver's door clicking shut.

"Penny?"

"Sorry, I must have fallen asleep. What did you find?"

"There are drag marks, possible shoe prints and some disturbance in the gravel too."

"Yes, I noticed all that myself. What do you think happened?"

"I don't want to speculate until we have the official cause of death, but to me it looks like blunt force trauma."

"You mean he was beaten?"

"Either that or he was hit by a car and someone moved the body in order to hide it."

"So it could have been an accident?"

John stared thoughtfully out of the window. "A slim chance. But I don't think it's likely. The fact the body was hidden is highly suspicious. Although if it had been an accident, then moving the body so as not to be caught is possible, I suppose. I'm just thinking out loud here, you understand? But my gut is telling me this was deliberate. Not to sound crass or unsympathetic, but I doubt the perpetrator would have reckoned on him being found so quickly. I know it was a childish idea coming to the cemetery, but if you hadn't, it could have been a long while before he was found. We can estimate the time of death within an hour or two as we know more or less the time he left the party. Or when he was last seen at least."

"Well, that's something I suppose," Penny said, hugging Fischer. She was feeling cold. Delayed shock, probably.

"I'll take you home now, Penny. We can take your statement in a day or two."

Penny breathed a sigh of relief. All she wanted to do was have a hot shower, curl up in her warm bed with Fischer resting on her feet and a good book in her hand to help her forget. She just hoped she wouldn't have nightmares.

FOUR

Penny awoke to the sound of bells tolling on Sunday morning. From the ones in Winstoke all the way through the villages. The sound of the bells reminded Penny of the churches. The churches made her think of the cemetery. Then her head filled with visions of Martin lying on the cold, wet earth the night before.

As though sensing her sudden distress, Fischer belly crawled up the duvet and licked her nose.

"Morning, little man," she said, giving him a hug. "Do you want your breakfast? Then we can go for a walk and have lunch with mum and dad."

Up on the top of Sugar Hill, Penny could see Winstoke Castle in the distance. The church bells had fallen silent long ago. She sent up a quiet prayer for Martin, then she and Fischer made their way back down the hill to the village.

Cherrytree Downs on a Sunday had a familiar and restful feel to it. As she walked through the streets, she could hear children playing somewhere. Their excited voices and laughter carrying on the cold air. Penny heard a radio playing from the kitchen of a house as she passed. No doubt preparations for a family Sunday lunch were taking place. The radio reminded her of Martin's garage, which she was approaching. It was closed now. Martin always had a pop music station playing in the dark recesses of the old place. Penny had spied it once, a small, grey transistor hanging from the rafters, suspended by a short length of clothesline. It was covered in grease and grime and its little speaker bravely punched out the sounds. But it was so tinny and distorted, Penny could never make out the tune. It was obviously company for the mechanic who'd worked alone day after day, for more years than Penny could count. Customers were always coming and going, but most of the time, Martin worked on his own. The place wouldn't be the same without him.

Penny recalled several people having issues with him at the party, but she couldn't understand why. Martin was the best mechanic in the area. He was dedicated and skillful. A professional who knew his way around an engine with his eyes closed. Who on earth would want to kill him? And surely it couldn't be over something as stupid as a car or a failed MOT?

"I wonder what will happen to the garage now, Fischer."

The Sunday tranquility was abruptly shattered as the thumping of bass notes of music rent the air. Penny jumped and Fischer started to bark as the loud beats continued, thumping at such a volume she could feel the beat in her chest. The dreadful racket was coming from Richard Sole's cottage.

It was All Saints Day and Penny knew she'd have to have the patience of all of them combined if she was to keep her temper. She approached the wrought-iron gate set in the high hedge and found Richard Sole standing on his doorstep. Large cigar in one hand and a bucks fizz in the other. He must have the central heating cranked up to its highest setting because he was dressed in a pair of brightly coloured shorts and a tee shirt.

He caught her eye and gave her a grin, cigar clamped between his teeth, and raised his glass in salute. Penny smiled politely.

"Do you think you could turn down your music, Richard? It is Sunday, after all." She shouted above the din.

There was a pause while he eyed her thoughtfully, and Penny thought he was going to refuse. But then he turned and slammed the door shut. It was an improvement, but the heavy base notes could still be felt and heard, albeit slightly muffled.

"I see you've been checking out that eyesore of a garage. Don't worry, I'll be pulling it down soon."

He grinned malevolently, then with a final puff of the cigar, which wreathed his head in smoke, opened his door, entered and slammed it shut behind him. A moment later, Penny heard the music cranked up a notch. She sighed and shook her head. What a rude and insufferable man Richard Sole was. Thank goodness his house was detached. As it was, she was pitying his nearest neighbours.

She and Fischer wandered on down the street and the cacophony faded, peace and tranquility restored.

She opened the gate to her parents' house and let Fischer off his lead. The door opened almost immediately and the

J. New

little dog launched himself at Sheila Finch, tail a blur and bottom wiggling, before barreling down the hall into the kitchen where his bowl was guaranteed to be filled with something delicious.

"Hello, love," Sheila said. "Come on in before we let all the heat out."

In the hallway, Penny was swept into a brief but fierce hug.

"Oh, Penny, we've heard about Martin. It's all round the village. What a dreadful shock. Your father is very cut up about it. But he won't talk. You know what your father's like."

"He'll talk in his own time, mum. He needs to come to terms with it."

"Yes, he's always been a deep thinker. Are you all right?"

"Much the same as you and dad I expect. Shocked and upset. I can't believe someone would kill Martin."

"Is John on the case?"

"Yes."

"And what about you? Are you helping him?" Before Penny could answer, Sheila went on. "I certainly hope so. Martin was one of our own, and no disrespect to John, but it needs someone who knew him and knows the village and the residents to find out who did this despicable thing."

"I'll do my best, mum," Penny smiled. "Is dad in the kitchen?"

"He's reading the paper in the lounge. Go on through, love, I'll put the kettle on."

Penny found her dad in his armchair, deep in the sports pages of the gazette.

40

News about the Winstoke cricket team was on the back page. The headline announced they were due to travel to a nearby town in the hopes a win would secure a promotion. The league, although still local amateur cricket, had more sponsorship from regional businesses and some of the players went on to try out for the county sides. If a young player put in a good run of innings for his county and was able to score regularly in the hundreds, it wouldn't be long before the national selectors took an interest.

"This is good news, Penny," her dad said, tapping the paper with his fingers.

"Hi dad," she said, giving him a kiss on the top of his head. "I don't really follow the cricket. I don't think I've been to a match since you took me when I was still at school."

"Well, we should fix that. If Winstoke gets promoted into the next league, we could go and watch their first home match. What do you say?"

"It's a bit cold to be standing on the boundary, dad."

"Not now, silly," Albert said, folding the paper and dropping it into the wooden magazine rack next to his chair. "If they move up a league, except for an important friendly coming up, they won't start playing until spring. You can call it my birthday present."

"Okay, dad. It's a deal. I'll even buy the tickets."

"They still have to win their promotion match, though, and from what I hear, the old bus is off the road." Albert's face clouded over as thoughts of the bus brought to mind the loss of the mechanic. Penny kept her mouth shut. Her dad would talk about it when he was ready. "They'll forfeit the game if they don't travel," Albert said.

"Penny, Albert, lunch is ready," Sheila called from the kitchen.

As usual, Sheila Finch had made enough food to feed a small army.

"Wow, mum, this looks amazing," Penny said, taking in the dishes of potatoes, steaming vegetables, miniature Yorkshire puddings and in pride of place in the centre, a delicious-looking nut roast.

"This is a new recipe," Sheila said, slicing the loaf and serving them all a couple of slices each. "Although I have adapted it a bit."

"It's excellent, mum. Don't you think so, dad?"

"It's very good. Mind you, your mum has always been an excellent cook, Penny."

"Oh, I enjoy it," Sheila said. "There's something very satisfying about making a full and healthy meal from scratch. It's much cheaper in the long run too. I don't think it's taught properly in schools nowadays, if at all. And it's even more important with how expensive everything is now. Did you know there are food banks in Winstoke, Penny? Isn't that dreadful? Of course there are some who can't help flaunt their wealth even in the face of other people's difficulties."

Penny frowned and glanced at her father, who shrugged. "Who do you mean, mum?"

"That lottery winner, Richard Sole. Do you know he has his meals delivered to him daily from a restaurant in town? What an utter waste of money. Personally, I think he should be helping those less fortunate than himself. But he's obviously a selfish individual with more money than sense."

"He won't have it for long if he keeps spending like that,"

Albert said, helping himself to more roast potatoes. "I've known it happen before. A Christmas bonus looks like a healthy windfall, but come the new year, it's all gone."

"Well, of course, a few hundred, or even a thousand pounds would go fast if you're not careful," Sheila said. "But we're talking about millions here, Albert. I can't even imagine what that amount of money looks like."

"Every time I hear someone talking about it, the amount seems to go up. Does anyone know how much he actually won?" Penny asked.

"It doesn't matter how much he won," Albert said. "It's what you do with it. It's all relative. You mark my words, it will be gone before the end of the summer if he spends it like water."

Penny couldn't believe that even though he'd bought the most expensive house in the village and appeared to have a new car delivered weekly, that he could be so profligate as to spend all that wealth so quickly. Could he?

"I saw him on my way here," Penny said. "Standing on his doorstep smoking a fat cigar and drinking bucks fizz. He was wearing shorts and his music was deafening. He said he was going to pull down the old garage."

"I saw him bullying Martin a few days ago," Sheila said. "He was very angry and very rude to poor Martin. Trying to get him to sell the place. But Martin was having none of it. He really was very calm and reasonable in the face of such animosity. Never raised his voice once. More placid than I would have been, that's for sure. I heard Martin tell him he would never sell. That he'd be working in the garage until the day he died."

The three of them sat in silence for a moment, considering the uncanny prescience of Martin's last words.

"Well, it looks like Richard Sole will get what he wants now," Albert said.

Yes, Penny thought. But did he commit murder to make it happen?

An hour later, after a slice of blackberry and apple crumble and a fresh pot of tea, it was time for Penny and Fischer to go home. It was only late afternoon, but the winter nights were drawing in and the dark clouds gathering on the horizon brought dusk all too soon.

Walking back, she was drawn to the illumination coming from Richard Sole's garage. Light was spilling out onto the driveway and inside she could see the red sports car he had been driving at the Halloween party. He was bent over the bonnet, but as Penny drew closer, she could see clearly the damage. The front light was broken and the metalwork bent.

Fischer gave a little bark and Sole started, spinning round to glare at her. Penny noticed he immediately shielded the damage to the car with his body, and retrieved the remote control to the garage door from his pocket. The door slowly closed, leaving them in twilight.

"What do you want?" he said sharply.

Penny shook her head and walked away. She wasn't going to waste her time with Richard Sole. Her parents were right. And so was Bishop John Bridges. 'A fool and his money are soon parted.'

FIVE

Monday dawned cold and frosty. Penny scraped the windscreen of the library van for the first time since the previous winter. Her breath formed billowing clouds in the cold morning air as she diligently cleared the windows of the thin layer of ice.

Fischer jumped in the passenger seat, ready to be off for their first day back at work. It was cold in the van and Penny shivered, but was incredibly pleased to see it was watertight and, turning the ignition key, relived when it started the first time. It wasn't long ago that Martin had given the van a full overhaul. He'd also been the one to obtain funding for the work as well as any more needed in the future. She had so much to thank him for. The old wagon, as he used to call it, was running perfectly. "She's put together well," he'd said with a smile. "She'll be trundling along these country roads for a long time yet. She'll probably outlast me."

They'd both laughed at the time. Penny looked back on

that exchange now with a deep sadness. Although neither of them could have known, his words had been painfully prophetic.

"Thank goodness we can't see into the future, Fish Face," Penny said now, wiping an errant tear from her cheek.

The little dog huffed in response.

Their first stop for the day was in Rowan Downs, a short drive but a pleasant one. She slowed down for a group of riders making their way to the bridal path. The horses' breath hanging in huge white plumes in the frigid air.

She'd almost reached the junction to the village when she was forced to hit the brakes hard as a car sped round the corner, ignoring the give way sign. The vehicle screeched to a halt and Trevor Smith, the taxi driver, got out. He shot Penny an angry look, shaking his head in annoyance.

Fischer gave a low growl, and Penny gave his ears a rub. Trevor walked round the back of his car and examined the rear light. It was broken and some of the body work crumpled. He turned and leaned on the car, shaking his head in mock exasperation while staring at Penny. A moment later, he walked over and tapped on her window. Penny rolled it down.

"I'm gonna need your insurance details, sweetheart," he said.

Penny was momentarily shocked into silence. But then rallied.

"What on earth are you talking about, Trevor?"

"You've run into the back of my car. What do you think I'm talking about? You can see the damage for yourself. You need to learn how a junction works, love."

"I know perfectly well how a junction works, thank you.

And you and I both know I was nowhere near your car. You ignored the give way sign and came tearing round a blind corner."

Penny looked at the road markings. Their instructions informed traffic approaching Rowan Downs to give way to those in the village. It was so clear Penny was at a complete loss as to how Trevor could suggest otherwise.

She sighed, and telling Fischer to stay put, climbed out of the van and went to survey the damage to Trevor's taxi. It had indeed taken a heavy knock. The break light cover was broken, with most of it missing. A large dent in the boot of the vehicle showed categorically he'd either been rear-ended at some point, but certainly not by her, or he'd reversed into something.

"Let me have your insurance details then, sweetheart. I haven't got time to mess about this morning," Trevor said, arms folded and foot tapping on the tarmac.

"Do you see any damage on my van, Trevor?" Penny said, pointing to the pristine front of her library. "No, of course you don't, because I never hit your car."

"Well, it's not too much damage, I suppose. Look, I'll let you off this time," he said in tones that suggested he was doing her a favour. "But be careful in future. Maybe it's time to take a refresher course and gen up on the highway code."

And with that hugely insulting final word, Trevor Smith got back in his taxi and drove off, leaving Penny staring after him open-mouthed.

A toot on a horn brought her back, and she realised she was blocking the road. She waved an apology to the driver and drove the final short distance to her spot for the day.

She was just pouring water on her tea when her friend, Mr Kelly, arrived. She offered to make him one, and he nodded.

"Thank you, Penny. I could do with a cuppa to warm myself up. It's certainly a cold one today. I heard your exchange with Trevor Smith," he said, once they'd settled in the two camping chairs. Fischer laying on Mr Kelly's feet.

"Don't worry, I can handle Trevor Smith."

"I've no doubt you can. But if you need a witness, I saw how he swerved in front of you. His car was already damaged. It looks as though he reversed into something hard. To be honest, I don't think the man should be driving at all. I'm quite sure he's drinking on the job. It's extremely dangerous, not to mention illegal. Do you know he went off the road and crashed his car recently?"

"No, I didn't know that," although Penny remembered now he'd said something about it at the Halloween party.

"Oh yes. I know he blamed it on poor Martin for shoddy work, which wasn't the case. Martin's work was always exemplary. I wouldn't be surprised if Trevor had actually been well over the limit and lost control. Look at the state of his current car. It's his new one, you know, and already it's bashed up."

"Trevor seems to blame everyone but himself when things go wrong, doesn't he?"

"Oh, nothing is ever his fault, Penny," Mr Kelly said in disgust. "Take his car as a case in point. Martin's work on the vehicle was excellent. As was all his work. Yet Trevor accused him of doing an inferior job because he had an accident while probably under the influence."

"But he wasn't the only one to accuse Martin of poor work recently, Mr Kelly. I overheard Harry Slade at the Halloween party saying much the same thing. I didn't believe a word of it. But why would he say it if it wasn't the case?"

"Well, he's another one who can't be trusted. There are rumours about the corruption within the cricket team. There is talk that Harry has been match fixing and then placing bets. He doesn't like to lose. When I was teaching, he spent more time in detention than at home. I remembering him throwing his cricket bat a fair few times in a fit of pique when the school team lost the match."

"I noticed he does have a temper on him."

Mr Kelly nodded and handed back his empty tea cup.

"So, what book can you recommend for me this week, Penny?"

Mr Kelly left, the latest thriller tucked under his arm, and within moments Penny found herself playing referee for Harriet Ward and Lillian Greaves. The two elderly ladies, best of friends although you wouldn't know it the way they constantly bickered, were in the midst of yet another squabble. This time over the best way to make bubble and squeak.

They occupied her for a good part of the morning and by the time they left, with new books and a new quarrel, Penny had just enough time to pack away and give Fischer a walk before heading off to the afternoon's appointment in Chiddingborne.

Fischer was snoozing on the camp chair in the van, his soft snores a comforting background noise. The crisp winter air nipped at Penny's cheeks as she sipped her warm tea, savoring its rich flavor. The distant chime of the village clock, combined with the soft rustling of the winter pansies outside the post office where she was parked for the afternoon, and the occasional chirping of a bird, added layers to the serenity of the moment. Penny often found solace in these quiet moments, with Fischer by her side and the comforting routine of her mobile library rounds. She cherished these brief respites, where she could lose herself in the beauty of the villages she served.

However, her peace was abruptly shattered when a shadow fell over her. She looked up from where she'd been crouched looking at the flowers, into the furious face of Harry Slade, his face red and veins popping at his temples. The sudden shift in the atmosphere was palpable, like a storm cloud passing overhead.

"What have you been saying about me?" Harry's voice was low, almost a growl.

"I've no idea what you mean, Harry," Penny replied, her voice steady despite the surprise. She straightened up, meeting his gaze squarely, her posture straight and defiant.

"You've been spreading malicious gossip. Lies." Harry's eyes darted around, as if searching for eavesdroppers.

Penny shook her head, genuinely baffled. "I've done no such thing. I have no reason to speak ill of you or anyone."

"I don't believe you. Everyone knows you spend your days snooping into other people's business. And I know you've been talking to that nosy parker Kelly, the old headmaster, about the cricket team. Whatever you think you know about me is complete rubbish, and I'll thank you not to go spreading lies about me, Penny Finch, or there'll be trouble."

Fischer, sensing the tension, lifted his head, his ears perked and eyes fixed on Harry. He let out a soft growl, protective of Penny, but didn't move from his seat.

Mrs Dodds and Claire Jewel, having heard the commotion, came out of their shops. They exchanged a quick glance, a silent agreement passing between them.

"Not him again," Claire whispered to Mrs. Dodds, her eyes narrowing.

"We can't let him bully Penny," Mrs. Dodds replied, determination evident in her voice.

"You leave Penny alone, Harry Slade. I've got my eye on you," Mrs Dodds said, stepping forward with a confidence that belied her age.

"So have I," Claire added, her voice firm. "Go away, Harry, and stop threatening Penny. She's not said a word about you."

Harry's eyes darted between the three women, realising he was outnumbered. "This isn't over, Penny," he hissed.

Harry gave the women a venomous look, his final ferocious gaze resting on Penny for a moment before he jabbed a warning finger in her direction and stalked off, muttering under his breath.

Once Harry was out of sight, Penny took a deep, steadying breath, her fingers instinctively seeking the soft fur of Fischer, who'd come to stand at her side. He nuzzled her hand in response. She wasn't intimidated by Harry Slade and would have been able to handle the situation herself, but she thanked the ladies for coming to her assistance, nonetheless.

"Think nothing of it, Penny," Mrs Dodds said, her voice softening. "You're not the only one talking about Harry Slade and his shady dealings. He can't carry on the way he is doing and not expect to get found out."

"But I haven't said a word about him," Penny reiterated, her confusion evident.

"Everyone knows he's been up to something," Claire said, her voice filled with unease. "He's got rid of most of the team and put in players he can trust. Those that are loyal only to him and let him get away with anything."

"The rumour is that he beat Martin to death with his cricket bat," Mrs Dodds said, lowering her voice and folding her arms. "Apparently Martin spoiled some scheme Slade had to get the team into a higher league and he lost his temper."

Claire nodded. "He's an out and out bully. Always looking for someone else to blame for his own mistakes."

Mrs Dodds turned to go back inside. "My William was chairman of the cricket club. I'll be having a word with him about this. And, Penny, don't let Harry Slade stop you from investigating, will you? You're good at it and Martin's murderer needs to be behind bars with the key thrown away. Between you and John, I'm convinced you'll solve it."

Penny nodded, hoping she looked a lot more confident than she felt. She took another sip of her tea, its warmth providing a small comfort against the chill of the confrontation. It dawned on her that Harry must have been eavesdropping on her conversation with Mr Kelly.

SIX

It was cold in Hambleton Chase the next morning, and Penny had settled comfortably on the camping stool inside the van. Fischer was fast asleep and dreaming on the front seat. No doubt chasing the rabbits he'd seen on their early morning walk. She wrapped her scarf tighter about her neck and plucked a random book off a nearby shelf. It was a collection of short stories set in a fantasy world, and she was drawn into the narrative immediately. She'd just guessed the young farmhand in the story was about to be accused of witchcraft when Gary Tate popped his head around the partially open side door.

"Morning, Gary." She laid the book on the driver's seat, making a note of the page number to return to later. "How can I help?"

He sighed heavily. "I was wondering if you had any books about getting a divorce?"

Penny clearly remembered the argument she'd witnessed between Gary and Cheryl at the Halloween party and how

Gary had walked away into the night alone. She'd felt pleased that he'd eventually found the courage to stick up for himself that night, but now she felt her heart contract as she studied Gary's hangdog expression. They'd been friends since school and she'd always known he'd had a soft spot for her, but while there was no romance, they had remained friends until the day Penny had left for university. By the time she returned, Cheryl was on the scene and her jealous and bullying nature put paid to any ideas Gary had of remaining friends with any other female.

"I don't have anything here," she said now. "But there are a number of books that I'm sure will help in the main library."

"I can't get into town today. There's too much to do at Thatchings. Cheryl was gone for most of yesterday. Lord knows where she was, leaving me to deal with everything myself."

"That's a lot to do on your own, especially if you're doing all the cooking. Your prowess as a chef is the reason the place has done so well, I'm sure of it."

"Maybe you could tell Cheryl that. She thinks I'm useless at everything."

Penny didn't know what to say. She'd heard Cheryl say that very thing to Gary on a number of occasions, as had most of the villagers, but it wasn't for her to intervene. She settled in to listen. It was obvious Gary needed someone to talk to, and it was the least she could do. She made him a cup of tea and they sat down. Penny waiting until he'd got his thoughts in order and was ready to speak.

"Things haven't been good between us for a long time. If I'm honest, they never were, really. It was great at the start,

54

but within a month I wanted to end it. But she wouldn't let me leave and the next thing I knew, we were married. I don't know how I got talked into it, but we've never really been happy."

"I'm sorry, Gary."

Fischer sprung up from the passenger seat and rested his paws on the back. Gary reached over to scratch the little dog's ears, a small smile appearing on his face as Fischer whined in ecstasy.

"She doesn't want me to leave this time, either."

"Perhaps that's a good sign. Maybe you can work out your issues if you sit and talk and be honest with one another. Perhaps she's realising she doesn't want to lose you?"

Gary shook his head. "I don't think it's me she doesn't want to lose. I think all she ever wanted was the business. There's no affection between us, there never has been to be fair, but she does know how to run a business, I'll give her that. It's much more profitable than when mum and dad were running it."

"You can tell me to mind my own business, Gary, but wouldn't the business be split between you if you divorced? Would you have to sell Thatchings and divide the assets?"

"Well, that's the reason she doesn't want a divorce. You see, the business isn't mine. It still belongs to mum and dad. As it is, me and Cheryl are employees. If we divorced, she wouldn't get anything. Although, maybe she could still keep her job. I don't know. The way things are, I don't think it would be a good idea."

"Would she want to stay in the area if you divorced? You've said she's a good business woman. I doubt she'd be out of a job for long. But if the relationship does end, I don't think you should worry about her too much, Gary. Perhaps you should concentrate on your own feelings and future. Do what's best for you for a change. What do your parents think?"

"I don't trouble them with business matters, Penny, and definitely not personal ones. They're too old and frail now. The last thing they need is to worry about what's going on with me. I came late in their lives as you know. Perhaps that's why I'm so old-fashioned in my ways. Cheryl calls me an old fuddy duddy. Maybe she's right."

"She's not right, Gary. Listen, why don't you come to the Pig and Whistle on a Thursday night for the quiz? At the moment, our team is John, Susie and me. We could do with a fourth member, and it will give you a change of scenery and a chance to relax a bit." Gary looked down and shook his head. "Oh, of course," Penny said. "It's not on this Thursday as it's Bonfire night. Are you going to the firework display and bonfire over at Hambleton Chase?"

"Not this year. Cheryl wants to have a meeting on Thursday night to discuss our future. I agreed, but all I want is for her to accept that I want a divorce. I need to move on."

"Well, maybe the Thursday after? You're welcome to join the team anytime."

Gary glanced at his watch. "Perhaps. Thank you. I'd better get on. I've been away too long as it is. I always get the silent treatment and dirty looks if I'm away too long. You should have seen the look she gave me after I'd got back home from the Halloween party. I thought she'd be furious I'd left her alone, but she looked shocked. I don't think she expected me to come back at all after what I said." He shrugged. "But where else would I go? Thatchings is my home."

"Of course it is. She can't expect you to leave your home, Gary. That wouldn't be fair at all. Do you want a book before you go? I find getting involved in a really good story is a great way to take my mind off things."

He shook his head. "I don't have time to read much at the moment. It's really busy during the day and it's late by the time I get to bed. I'm usually asleep before my head hits the pillow."

"Are you walking back?"

"Yes. I tend to walk most of the time as she only lets me have the car when I'm buying supplies from the wholesalers. Thanks for the tea."

He zipped up his jacket, patted Fischer and stepped out of the van, giving Penny a last wave before trudging back through the village. He had a bit of a walk ahead of him. The bed-and-breakfast was a little way out of the village, about a mile from where Penny was now. But he was obviously used to it. She watched him, shoulders hunched and head down, as he disappeared from sight. She hoped the meeting between him and his wife would go well, but somehow doubted it would.

That same evening, Penny had just settled down to watch one of her favourite Agatha Christie films with Fischer curled up on the sofa next to her, when her phone rang. It was Susie. She pressed pause on the remote.

"Hi, Susie." She could hear muffled voices in the background and assumed Susie was talking to Tom.

"Hi, Penny. Sorry about that. Tom's just going to the shop for some wine."

"No problem. How are things?"

"Pretty good, actually. I've no idea how long this thing with Tom is going to last, but I'm enjoying it while I can."

"Is he living with you?"

"Good grief, no. He's lodging with someone over in Hambleton Chase, but has been staying here while the kids are with their father. Anyway, I've got a bit of news for you. I've been investigating the rumours of cricket match fixing for the paper and Tom and I saw something interesting recently. In fact, Tom took photos. I'll send them on to you. We were following Harry Slade and saw him have a meeting with a man in a motorway service station car park."

"Do you know who it was?" Penny asked.

"Not at first. But I've been doing a bit of digging, and it turns out he's the captain of the other cricket team. The one they're playing for the promotion. We saw Harry hand over a brown envelope. I'm convinced he's up to his neck in match fixing. I've also seen him enter several different betting shops, and I'm pretty sure he's also putting wagers on the matches."

"Is that allowed?" Penny wasn't sure about the rules around sports. The local cricket team weren't in the big leagues. Predominantly filled with amateur players, it was actually small fry in the scheme of things, but she knew it was run to a professional standard. However, betting on the outcome of a game you were involved in as a player and captain didn't sound legitimate.

"No, it's not legal at all," Susie said. "And if the team are promoted, they will be playing with semi-professionals. It's a much bigger deal, Penny, and consequently there's more money involved. I think Slade is giving financial bribes to the other side to forfeit the game so he can make more cash betting on a bigger league."

"It sounds as though you're really getting your teeth into this investigation, Susie."

"I am. My editor is very happy for me to explore all the avenues. He's a huge cricket fan and is furious with the possibility of match fixing. If it's true, he wants to see Harry Slade in the dock. Tom's photos have been really useful in gathering evidence."

"You know I trust your judgement, Susie, but that envelope could have contained anything. Something innocent, like special dietary requirements for the match teas or something?"

Susie laughed. "I get your point, but Harry could have emailed that information. Why go to the trouble of meeting in a service station car park miles from anywhere if it was all above board? Besides, if you'd been there and witnessed it, you'd have come to the same conclusion, Penny. It was the look on their faces. They were definitely up to no good." Penny heard the door slam in the background. "That's Tom back, Penny, I'd better go. I'll send the photos to you later."

"Okay, thanks, Susie. Have a good night."

Penny ended the call and pressed play on the remote, once again settling down to watch her film, but the conversation with Susie was playing over and over in her mind and she found she couldn't concentrate on the exotic scenes of Egypt on the screen.

Penny knew how good Susie was at her job. She had an excellent instinct for winkling out illicit activity and if she was convinced Harry Slade was involved in match fixing, then she was inclined to believe her. But how did that relate to the death of Martin? Or was it something entirely unconnected? There was the issue with the cricket team bus. Harry had been apoplectic at the Halloween party. But surely an unroadworthy team bus wasn't something you'd kill someone over? But then again, Susie had intimated there were vast sums of cash involved and more to come if the team were promoted. The lack of transport could mean forfeiting the next match and therefore could potentially lose Harry a lot of money, and by the sounds of it, a regular revenue source. Perhaps they were connected. She needed to do a bit more investigation herself.

SEVEN

The biting cold of the morning was a stark reminder that winter was settling in. Penny awoke, her nose feeling like it had been left in a freezer overnight. Beside her, Fischer, ever the opportunist, had managed to sneak under the covers, seeking warmth. His gentle snores were a testament to his comfort.

She scratched behind his ears. A morning ritual they both enjoyed. "Come on, little man, time to get up."

Fischer's tail wagged beneath the duvet, betraying his feigned slumber. Penny chuckled, "Pretending to be asleep doesn't work if your rear end is wiggling, Fish Face."

With a sigh, she braced herself for the cold, grabbing her dressing gown and slipping her feet into her warmest slippers. Fischer, ever eager, had already bounded out of bed and made his way downstairs, waiting impatiently by the back door, his tail thumping in anticipation.

After a hearty breakfast, porridge for her and an extra portion of biscuits for Fischer to combat the cold, they prepared to set out.

Penny's mobile library, with its vibrant lime-green exterior and white roof, was a familiar and beloved sight in the villages she served. As she drove towards Holts End, the van's engine hummed a comforting tune, blending with the soft melodies of the radio. Fischer, perched on the passenger seat, looked out of the window, his nose twitching at the myriad scents carried by the cold wind.

The journey between villages was Penny's thinking time. The rhythmic motion of the van, combined with the picturesque English countryside, provided the perfect backdrop for reflection. Today, her thoughts were dominated by the case. Martin's sudden death had sent shock-waves through the tight-knit community, and the weight of finding answers pressed heavily on her.

As she approached Holts End, Penny's thoughts shifted to the upcoming lunch with Susie. Their weekly meet-ups were more than just a meal; they were a tradition. From sharing the latest village gossip to discussing personal challenges, these lunches were a cherished respite from their busy lives. And today, Penny hoped Susie might have some information or insight into the case.

Parking the van in its usual spot, Penny was greeted by a group of eager readers. The first was Mrs Prewitt, her soft white hair neatly tied in a bun, a few stray curls framing her face. Despite the cold, her bright blue eyes sparkled with mischief and anticipation. She was wrapped in a thick woolen cardigan, the kind that looked like it had been lovingly hand-knitted, and her sensible shoes clicked softly on the pavement.

Around her neck, the familiar locket glinted in the morning light. It had been a gift from her late husband, she'd told Penny, and she never took it off.

"Ah, Penny!" Mrs. Prewitt exclaimed, tapping her wooden cane on the ground for emphasis. "Do you have any of those romance novels? The ones where the characters are, you know... my age?"

Penny chuckled, "Good morning, Mrs. Prewitt! Looking for some seasoned romance, are we?"

Mrs. Prewitt leaned in, her voice taking on an animated tone, "Well, just because we're old doesn't mean we don't like a little flutter in the heart! Especially with this cold weather, I need something to warm me up from the inside."

Penny grinned. "I've got just the thing for you. And I promise, no teenagers in sight."

Mrs. Prewitt let out a delighted chuckle. "Oh, you always know just what I'm looking for. The type of thing like in Chapter 12 of 'Summer's End,' when the protagonist finds her long-lost love in the most unexpected place."

Penny laughed. "I know exactly the type of the thing. I'll keep it in mind when I'm sorting out the books for next week, Mrs Prewitt."

Mrs. Prewitt's expression softened, and she gently took Penny's hand. "Penny," she said with genuine concern, "I'm so sorry about Martin. What dreadful news! It's a cruel twist of fate. But remember, even in the darkest tales, dawn eventually comes."

Penny nodded. "Thank you Mrs Prewitt."

"Until next week, my dear."

Fischer had begun performing his tricks, drawing a crowd

of admirers. Penny smiled, watching him. His antics, from simple sit-and-stay commands to more complex routines, never failed to entertain. And today, it seemed he was in his element, basking in the attention and treats showered upon him.

As the morning progressed, Penny found herself engrossed in conversations with the villagers. From recommending books to discussing local events, the library was abuzz with activity.

"Good morning, Mr Gilbert." Penny greeted her next customer.

"Ah, Penny," Mr. Gilbert began, his deep voice filled with warmth. "I've been looking for a new adventure novel. Something to take my mind off things. Preferably where the hero isn't using one of those newfangled phones to solve everything."

Penny smiled. "Of course, Mr. Gilbert. I've got a few new arrivals that might interest you. Heroes who rely on their wits and not just technology."

He stroked his beard thoughtfully, "That's what I like to hear. I remember the good old days when maps didn't talk back to you. You know, I heard about Martin. Such a tragedy. He wasn't around when I still had my car, but I've heard good things about his work. And he always greeted you when you walked by his garage."

Penny nodded. "Yes, it's been tough for everyone. Martin was well-liked."

Mr. Gilbert sighed. "I miss driving, you know. Gave it up as age caught up with me. There's a certain freedom to it. But, I suppose, there's also a sort of freedom in a good book. Takes you to places without ever leaving your chair."

Penny handed him a thick tome. "I think you'll like this one. It's about a sea voyage. Reminds me a bit of 'Moby Dick'."

Mr. Gilbert chuckled, "Ah, Melville. Now there's a tale. Thank you, Penny. And keep your chin up. The village is rooting for you and Detective Inspector Monroe to solve this dreadful business."

All morning in the back of her mind, the case had loomed large, but it wasn't until there was a brief lull that Penny's thoughts returned to the suspects. Richard Sole, with his newfound wealth and brash demeanor, was hard to ignore. His overt interest in acquiring Martin's garage and his lack of integration into the community made him stand out. But was he capable of murder?

Then there was Trevor. He'd been the local taxi driver for years. His struggles with alcohol and the potential loss of his livelihood added layers of complexity to his character. But could he have taken such a drastic step?

The last on Penny's list was Harry Slade. The obnoxious bully. Just thinking about him made her blood boil.

"Goodness, that's a frightening face," a voice said at the library door.

"Oh, Clara," Penny said. "Sorry, I was just thinking."

"Martin's death weighing heavily, is it?"

Penny nodded. Clara, wrapped in layers of vibrant scarves and a deep blue coat, gave Penny a sympathetic look. She was a well-known figure in the village, not just for her eclectic fashion sense, but also for her art. Clara had a unique talent for capturing the essence of stories in her sketches. While she often drew scenes inspired by books, she was careful never to replicate copyrighted material directly. Instead, she created abstract interpretations, capturing the emotions and themes of the stories, which were always in high demand at local art shows.

"I'm feeling the pressure to solve this one quickly."

"I can tell," Clara said softly, her eyes scanning Penny's face. "You always have that intense look when something's bothering you. Try not to let it take over, Penny. I know how important Martin was to you, to all of us, but you must think about your sanity and your health."

"I will, Clara. So, what are you looking for this week?"

Clara's reading was as eclectic as her dress. Anything from thrillers to non-fiction art books.

"Something set in the regency era. Romance, mystery, epic family saga, I don't mind. I need to immerse myself in that time for a stained glass window I've been commissioned to do."

"Wow, that sounds interesting. I have all of Jane Austen's work and some of Lord Byron's poetry. Would they work?"

"Probably not Byron, but I'll take the first two Jane Austens, please."

With her books tucked under her arm, Clara squeezed Penny's hand, telling her once again to take care of herself, then disappeared in a waft of heady perfume and a rustle of fabric.

With the morning session behind her, Penny closed the library and gave Fischer his lunch and walk, before heading to Thistle Grange. She parked in her usual spot, then she and her little dog walked over to The Pot and Kettle for her weekly lunch date with Susie.

The Pot and Kettle had always been a cozy haven, but today, the remnants of Halloween added an extra layer of charm. Faded orange and black streamers hung from the wooden beams, and a few carved pumpkins, their grins now slightly wilted, adorned the window sills, each with a tea light candle inside, their flames dancing and casting a warm, golden hue.

In one corner, a makeshift scarecrow, dressed in old farmer's clothes, sat propped up on a chair, a straw hat tilted over its button eyes. Beside it, a small table held a glass jar filled with leftover sweets, a sign inviting patrons to help themselves. The soft glow of fairy lights, intertwined with faux cobwebs, draped across the walls, cast playful shadows. The faint hum of a jazz tune played in the background, a stark contrast to the spooky ambiance. The scent of cinnamon and roasted coffee beans wafted through the air, mingling with the earthy aroma of the carved pumpkins.

It was like a small piece of nirvana to Penny, who, after taking a deep breath, felt the nervous tension, which had been with her ever since she'd found Martin's body, calm and settle. She couldn't help but smile as she noticed a group of elderly ladies at a nearby table, their conversation animated as they discussed their Halloween experiences. One of them held up a hand-knitted scarf, its pattern inspired by a spider's web, proudly showing it off to her friends. Another, not to be outdone by her lunch companion, pulled from her shopping bag a black knitted hat with a huge plump spider sitting on the top. They all took turns to wear it, dissolving in fits of giggles like teenagers.

The place was busy, but a table had been reserved for Penny and Susie under the cast iron spiral staircase leading to the upstairs seating area. She removed her big coat and took a seat under the dark leaves of a tall rubber plant. Fischer made himself comfortable under the table with his chin on his paws and watched the goings on in the cafe.

"Has Susie not arrived yet?" She asked the waitress, who'd come with a bowl of water for Fischer.

"Not yet. I haven't seen her since you were both in last week."

Penny thought that was a bit odd. Susie was always here first. But recently, since she'd been seeing Tom, her friend had been rushed and run late on more than one occasion.

She ordered tomato soup with fresh from the oven, crusty bread and a dish of local butter. The warm aroma of the tomato soup wafted up to Penny's nostrils, instantly transporting her back to her childhood. The tangy richness, complemented by a hint of fresh basil, was very similar to her mother's cherished recipe. One that had been handed down from her own mother, Penny's Gran. She'd almost finished when Susie came barreling through the door. Her hair was a chaotic mess and her outfit was disheveled. Penny noticed with a wry smile that her coat had been buttoned up wrong.

She gave Penny an apologetic smile and darted to the counter to order coffee. "Strong with extra sugar, please."

Susie sat down, breathless. She hung her bag over the back of the chair, which instantly tumbled to the floor. She put her hands over her face and let out a sign of frustration, followed by a growl which turned into a pitiful moan.

"Late night?" Penny asked.

"Yes."

"Too much wine? Should you be driving, Susie?"

"I didn't have much more to drink after I spoke to you." She groaned again and looked at Penny. "We talked," she said in a heavy and sombre tone. "I asked what he wanted from our relationship."

"Oh, Susie, you didn't."

"I know, I know. I'm an idiot. I got all serious and ruined the fun."

"What was his reaction?"

"He was very understanding, actually. Told me not to worry. But I couldn't help thinking about the age difference. I think he does like me, Penny, but if I'm honest with myself, I was probably trying to scare him off. Especially after what I saw on his phone."

"What do you mean?"

"It was when I was searching for those photos to send you."

"Which you still haven't done."

"Haven't I? Sorry, Penny. Hang on, let me have a look. Oh, what an idiot I am. I sent them to myself. I obviously wasn't thinking straight. I'll send them to you now." She found Penny's number and quickly forwarded the images. Putting her phone on the table with a thud, she looked back at Penny. "I found a load of images of his ex-girlfriend. She's really stunning, Penny, and young. There was this one picture. They were at a beach, sun setting, looking so... perfect. It just made me question everything."

"Well, that hardly means anything. He's a photographer. If they were good shots, then he could be keeping them for his portfolio. Besides, I bet if a look through mine I'll find a few of Edward. I never think to delete photos from my phone. It doesn't mean anything."

Susie stirred her coffee, deep in thought.

"I expect you're right, Penny, but I don't know if I can be with someone who is thinking of another woman. I've done it once already, remember. James was obviously thinking of someone else before he left. I can't do it again."

"I understand that, Susie, but you didn't know that until after the fact. Tom isn't keeping it a secret from you, is he? You know he's had girlfriends in the past and if he was keeping secrets he wouldn't let you use his phone, would he?"

Susie frowned. "No, I suppose not. So you think I'm blowing this out of all proportion?"

Penny smiled. "Just a bit. I know it's difficult for you, it's the first real relationship you've had since James went, and having been left once, I don't mean that to sound harsh by the way, you are automatically going to assume it will happen again. Understandable, but not necessarily true. I think you're sabotaging your chance of happiness with Tom by comparing him to your ex-husband. They aren't the same person, Susie, and it's not fair on either of you. Try to relax a bit and take each day as it comes. Have some fun together. It might not last, but at least you can enjoy what time you do have."

Penny felt Fischer stand and a paw suddenly landed on her knee.

"I think Fischer needs to go out, Susie. Order me a tea, will you? I'll be right back. And try not to worry."

Penny stepped out with Fischer into the bustling Cobbler's Lane, a picturesque street lined with a mix of quaint shops and charming cafes, each with their own unique facade. The lane was a blend of the old and the new, where vintage signage hung above modern storefronts, and the soft hum of chatter filled the air. As they made their way around to the back of the shops, the atmosphere shifted, the quaint charm giving way to a more rustic, untouched feel. Its ground was uneven and marked with the playful remnants of the recent children's ghost walk from the Halloween festivities.

A few forgotten paper ghosts fluttered gently from the low branches of the overhanging trees, and chalk drawings of spooky figures still adorned the ground, now smudged by the passage of numerous feet.

Across from the buildings, a dense hedgerow stood tall, its foliage a mix of autumnal colours separating the lane from a sprawling field. This open space was a haven for local riders, who kept their horses in a quaint, private stable nestled at the far end. The field, dotted with makeshift obstacles for training, was a playground for both seasoned and novice riders. The gentle neighing of horses and the distant thud of hooves against the earth added to the village ambiance.

Fischer was energetically sniffing along the line of buildings, his nose twitching with every new scent he discovered. His tail wagged with enthusiasm as he explored the myriad smells the back alley offered. Penny gently steered him towards the hedgerow, allowing him to mark his territory. However, once he'd completed his business, something seemed to catch his attention. With a sudden burst of focus, he veered back towards the walls, pulling Penny along with an urgency in his scamper. His nose was glued to the ground as he followed a particular scent trail with single-minded determination along the row of buildings.

"What is it, Fischer?" Penny said, trotting to keep up with him.

Penny could feel the excitement in the dog's movements, the way his body tensed with anticipation with each step. This wasn't unusual for Fischer; his keen sense of smell often led them on mini-adventures. However, this time, the intensity of his focus was different. Penny's heart raced a tad faster as she allowed Fischer to lead the way, her grip on the lead firm yet allowing him the freedom to explore. His behavior was a silent signal to her that he might be onto something interesting, possibly significant. He'd done it before. More than once.

As they approached the back of the old furniture shop, Fischer's pace quickened, his nose glued to a trail that led straight to a partially open window. His tail wagged with a fervor that Penny had come to recognise as the prelude to a discovery.

With a sudden leap, Fischer propped his front paws onto the windowsill, his body quivering with anticipation. His whines of urgency echoed off the old brick walls, drawing Penny's attention to a rag caught on the inside catch of the window, its end fluttering gently in the breeze.

"What have you found, Fish Face?" Penny murmured, her curiosity roused. She reached up and freed the rag, half expecting it to be covered in secret writing or something. But as she held the rag in her hands, her initial excitement waned. It was just an old, grimy piece of cloth, obviously torn from something larger and stained with what looked like food.

Fischer's nose nudged at the rag in her hand, his eyes bright and expectant. Penny couldn't help but feel a pang of disappointment. She had hoped for a clue, a lead, something that would propel her investigation forward. But all they had was a filthy scrap of fabric.

She examined it closer, trying to understand Fischer's interest. There was nothing extraordinary about it, nothing that screamed 'clue' to her. Yet Fischer was still fixated on it, his nose twitching as he sniffed the air around the rag.

Penny sighed, "Well, it seems like this rag holds secrets only discernible to your keen nose, little man. It must be the smell of food." She stuffed it into her pocket. She'd dispose of it later and gave Fischer a biscuit.

It was a small mystery, and she had a much bigger and more pressing one to solve. She secured the window, ensuring it was shut tight to prevent any unwarranted entry or exit, then led Fischer back towards the cafe.

Penny returned to find Susie staring into her coffee cup, her fingers absentmindedly tracing the rim. The usual spark in her eyes seemed dimmed, replaced by a veil of fatigue. Her laughter lines seemed to deepen with the weight of her thoughts.

"The coffee isn't working, I take it?" Penny said, throwing her coat over the back of her chair and settling Fischer. She poured herself a cup of tea and looked at her friend over the rim of the cup.

"Not really. I'm exhausted," Susie sighed, her voice carrying a hint of defeat. She looked up, attempting a smile that didn't quite reach her eyes.

Penny reached across the table, giving her friend's hand a reassuring squeeze. "It's emotional too, as well as lack of sleep."

"Yes, I know. I just want this day to be over so I can go home and go straight to bed. The kids are with their father for one more night, so I should have recovered my energy by then. I hope."

Penny smiled, trying to lighten the mood. "Just in time for the bonfire and fireworks at Hambleton Chase. You are taking them?"

"Absolutely. The kids have been looking forward to it. One day, when I'm old and grey, they can take me," Susie said, a hint of her usual humor peeking through.

Penny grinned. "No doubt I'll be with you. We'll be like Harriet and Lillian from Rowan Downs."

Susie laughed, the sound a comforting melody to Penny's ears. "Good grief, now there's a thought. Although, hopefully, we won't be arguing as much as those two do."

Susie's phone buzzed abruptly on the table, startling them both. She picked it up and her face turned pale as she read the message. "Oh no, I completely forgot! I have a meeting with a source for the story I'm working on. I was supposed to be there twenty minutes ago!"

She scrambled to her feet, her chair screeching against the floor. "Penny, I'm so sorry, I have to dash. We'll catch up later, promise!"

Without waiting for a response, she grabbed her coat, threw some money on the table for her coffee, and rushed out of the cafe. Penny watched in concern as her friend dashed down the lane towards her car. Susie had fought a hard battle to get the promotion to senior reporter at the paper, and she was really good at her job. But this new relationship with Tom was putting it all at risk. Late nights, childish jaunts around cemeteries in the dark, forgetting appointments at work. None of this was like Susie, and Penny was really worried about her friend. She hoped she'd see sense before it was too late.

Penny paid the bill and after saying goodbye to the staff and a few of the patrons she knew, she and Fischer went back to work.

Penny wasn't even halfway back to the library when Fischer started straining at the lead and giving excited little yips. She looked up and smiled. John was waiting outside the van. She let her little dog off and watched him race up to his favourite person, climbing up his trouser leg, his tail a blur of canine excitement. John lifted him up and got a full face wash for his pains.

"Somebody is glad to see me," he said when Penny arrived.

"We both are," she replied, leaning in for a kiss. "So, how is the investigation going?" she asked, once they were inside the warmth of the van, the kettle boiling in the background.

Monroe pulled a face. "It's a slog, if I'm honest. One step forward, two steps back. It's frustrating and exhausting. Trying to keep my team motivated and positive when we're hitting constant brick walls is draining, to put it mildly. Martin was killed during one of the busiest times of the year, so sifting through all the party goers trying to find eyewitnesses who actually saw something relevant is like trying to find the proverbial needle in a haystack."

"I can imagine," she said, handing him a cup.

"Thanks, Penny. Just what I need to warm me up. It's freezing out there."

Penny sat on the other camp chair, Fischer at her feet and still looking adoringly at John. "So you've made no headway at all?"

"I didn't say that," he grinned, his eyes lighting up. "I did witness one row at the party, as you know, so we're digging deeper into that. Plus, we have a few 'persons of interest' we're keeping tabs on. At the moment, with the murder happening so close to the road, our initial thoughts are it was possibly a hit and run. Then they moved the body to where you found it. That's what the drag marks seem to indicate. I'm waiting for the full report from the pathologist. I hope you understand there's only so much I can share with you, though."

Penny felt a sharp sting in her chest as John referred to Martin as 'the body'. It was a cold, impersonal term for someone who had been warm, vibrant, and a dear friend. She looked away for a moment, fighting back the tears that threatened to spill. She understood the detachment was necessary for John's work, but it still hurt.

"I'm so sorry, Penny," he said, reaching out and squeezing her knee affectionately. "I didn't mean that to sound so crude. I worry about you, you know. This case, it's hitting too close to home," he said, his eyes searching hers for any sign of distress. "I know Martin was a friend and you're feeling his loss. Are you all right? I should have asked before now."

"It's all right, John, honestly," Penny said, reaching out to lift Fischer, who, concerned about her tears, was trying to get onto her knee. "I know you have to keep your emotions out of an investigation, otherwise you'd go mad. And yes, it's very hard because Martin was a friend, but that's the reason I'm all the more determined to help solve it." She took a deep breath. "So you're looking for damage to cars?"

"Among other things, yes. Have you seen something?"

"A couple of things, actually. I'd been visiting mum and dad and walked by Richard Sole's place. He was in the garage and didn't see me at first. When he did, he closed the garage door pretty sharpish. But I'd seen some damage to his car. It was the red one he was driving on Halloween."

John had taken out his notebook and was busy scribbling. "And the second thing?"

"It was Monday morning, and I was just on my way to work when Trevor Smith swerved in front of me from a blind corner. He stopped and got out, accusing me of hitting his car. I hadn't, of course, but there was some damage to the back of his vehicle. Mr Kelly saw and heard the whole thing if you need a witness."

John nodded. "Was the damage to Smith's vehicle recent, do you think?"

Penny thought back for a moment, then sighed. "To be honest, I don't remember. I was just furious he'd accused me of something I hadn't done. It wouldn't surprise me if he's done that sort of thing before and got away with it. Maybe agreeing to hush it up or not get the insurance companies involved and forfeit a no claims bonus by agreeing to compensation in cash. I don't know this for certain, of course, but it's the sort of money making racket I wouldn't put past him. But, thinking about it now, the damage was to the back of his car, not the front, like you'd expect if he'd hit someone."

"Unless he pulled in front, signalling he was available. It's a taxi, remember?"

"What, and then reversed into Martin, killing him?" Penny's voice trembled with shock.

"I know, it's a grim thought. But it's a possibility we can't ignore, unfortunately."

"You've spoken to Trevor, I assume?"

"I've spoken to him, Slade and Sole."

"And?"

"They've all provided alibis, though I'm skeptical. It's all 'friends of friends' vouching for each other. But there's something off. I can sense it. They're hiding something. For one thing, they were all extremely nervous when I spoke to them. Whether it's something to do with Martin's death or some other crime they're involved in, I can't tell. But rest assured, I will find out. Your idea about Trevor is a good one. I'll do it bit more research on that."

"Could they be in it together, do you think?" Penny asked. "I know it seems a bit far-fetched, but if they'd conspired to kill Martin, then no one person would be to blame. All of them had something to gain by getting rid of him."

John looked up for a moment, gazing out the window, thinking. Penny wondered if her suggestion hadn't crossed his mind. She waited.

"It's certainly something to think about and explore further if needed. Thank you, Penny. Now I really must go."

He stepped out of the van and she followed. He drew her in and kissed her, murmuring into her hair. "I'll see you later."

"Oh, before you go, Susie and Tom did a bit of sleuthing recently."

John chuckled, "Great, as if having Miss Marple wasn't enough. Now I've got Tommy and Tuppence on my hands too."

Penny grinned at John's wry smile.

"I'm sure Susie will be thrilled you're calling her Tuppence. Actually it's about Harry Slade. He met someone in suspicious circumstances recently and they took photos. Susie was following the lead about his match fixing and is now convinced he's betting on the outcomes of the games. And making quite a bit of money, by all accounts. He gave someone an envelope. Susie eventually identified them as the captain of the opposite cricket team. I'll forward the pictures to you now."

John looked at his phone as it pinged.

"Got them. Well, that's certainly interesting. I'll pass it on to the right department. Thanks Penny."

He gave her another quick kiss, rubbed Fischer's head, then dashed off.

EIGHT

There was always an air of the weekend being just around the corner for Penny on a Thursday, as it was her last working day of the week. She was also based in her own village in the morning, which meant a slight lie in. In the afternoon she went to the main library in Winstoke, spending the time stocking up for the following week, and catching up on the gossip with her colleagues Sam and Emma.

This Thursday there was also a bubble of additional excitement as it was Bonfire Night, also known as Guy Fawkes night, and there was to be the big annual event with a firework display at Hambleton Chase sports field.

"Remember, remember the fifth of November," she said to herself as she made her morning tea. "Gunpowder treason and plot."

To commemorate the foiling of the plot by Guy Fawkes to blow up the houses of parliament in 1605, it amazed Penny that the celebration was still held over 400 years later. And not just in England, but in other countries that were part of the British Empire at the time. The fireworks, a major part of the celebration, were representations of the explosives that Guy Fawkes and his cohorts never got to use.

"Right then, little man," she said to Fischer. "Ready for work?"

Fischer gave a woof and ran to grab his lead.

She'd parked up at her usual spot by the village green and was gathering the books her regulars had requested when her first two visitors of the day arrived. Two children Penny knew very well. Ellen and Billy Hughes, Susie's kids. Fischer ran up to them and received huge hugs and an even bigger fuss.

"Penny for the guy," Ellen said in a sing-song voice, pulling the go cart nearer the camper van door. She then burst out laughing at the unintended joke. Then Billy started. Penny grinned.

"If I really did have a penny for every time someone has said that to me, I'd be living in a mansion. So, this is your guy? He looks great. Did you make him yourselves?" The kids nodded, obviously proud of their efforts, and rightly so. "Mind you, I think I recognise his head?"

"It's King Charles," Billy said with a grin. "I made it for the Queen's Birthday parade. Mummy said she didn't mind if I used it for the guy."

"Well, it looks excellent. Where did you get his clothes?"

The guy was made from an old pair of trousers that had been knotted with string at the ankles. A pair of battered old trainers had been loosely attached to the bottom. The blouse had definitely seen better days and, like the trousers, had been unevenly stuffed with scrunched up newspaper. One arm was fatter than the other and the buttons were bulging out, newspaper poking out between them. It was a ragged affair, with a large piece missing from the hem. Penny thought the trousers were an old pair of Billy's, as were the trainers, but the blouse looked familiar as well. It was possible it was one that Susie no longer had a use for, but it didn't look like her style at all. Fischer came over and began to sniff at this very odd person.

"My trousers and trainers," Billy said.

"Mummy found an old shirt and said we could use it. It's perfect. What do you think?"

"I think it's the best guy I've ever seen. Now, I don't have a penny." The kids looked crestfallen. "But I do have a pound each."

"Yay. Thank you, auntie Penny."

"So, what are you going to spend it on? There will be lots of stalls at the bonfire tonight."

Ellen shook her head solemnly and deposited the pound in a collection tin nestled between the guy's feet. Billy did likewise. Penny had missed the tin.

"It's for the homeless people," he said.

Ellen nodded. "We saw a homeless lady when we were on holiday with dad. I wanted to give her some money, but dad's girlfriend said she was probably richer than they were and didn't really need it."

"She looked sad," Billy said. "And dirty."

Ellen nodded. "I don't think she was pretending. I told mummy, and she said we should use our guy to help so we can give the money to charity."

"That's such a great idea. I'm so proud of you both."

She bent to give them a big hug each. "And if you find me

at the bonfire tonight, I'll pop a bit more in your collection box."

"Now then, who is this?" a voice said.

"Hello, Mrs Evans. Penny for the guy?" Ellen said.

"They're collecting for a homeless charity," Penny said.

"What a very nice thing to do. Why don't you pop over to the bakery and wait for me? I'll give you some money for your guy then. I think I might have some jam donuts fresh from the oven too. I always make too many."

Penny watched them both, deep in thought, as they hurriedly pulled the cart across the green, eager for Mrs Evans' jam donuts. What was it she had seen or heard recently that she'd just been reminded of?

"Penny?"

"Oh, sorry, Mrs Evans, I was miles away. You've come for your book. Hang on, I'll just get it for you."

It was the latest in a series of crime novels which, having just discovered them, the baker couldn't get enough of. Penny had started the first herself on Mrs Evans' recommendation, and she was reading them almost as fast. Once she'd left, book tucked under her arm, Penny watched the children exit the shop a few moments later. Huge jammy grins on the faces. They stopped briefly and waved to Penny, then disappeared round the corner. Penny smiled at the thought of the look on Susie's face when they arrived back home. No doubt she'd be getting a flannel to scrub their faces ready for school.

She was kept busy for the morning, so didn't have much time to think about what had triggered a sudden memory. It was something important, but was proving elusive.

Eventually, it was time to shut the library, take Fischer for his walk and then drive over to Winstoke. But before she did, she had one last errand to run.

Like a lot of dogs, Fischer did not like fireworks. She'd had a chat with the vet at The Rough Spot and he'd recommended a calming tablet, which she could buy over the counter at the pharmacy. It was a herbal one rather than a pharmaceutical, which Penny was pleased to note, and it had worked a treat last year.

Outside, the pharmacy retained a quaint, old-world charm with its vintage signage and the two giant, weird-shaped glass bottles in the window. The bottles, filled with bright red and green liquids, seemed to be relics from a bygone era, stirring a sense of nostalgia in Penny. She assumed they were coloured water now, but they had been there since she'd been a child, and she'd always imagined they were some sort of witch's brew when she'd been young.

She pushed open the door and the electronic chime rang out, activated by her walking through a sensor. It was the only indication of a modern update as the inside looked as it always had done. It was a blend of the past and present. The wooden shelves, laden with an array of medicines, ointments, and old apothecary jars, stood against the walls, while the modern cash register sat incongruously on the vintage counter. It even smelled the same. The familiar scent of antiseptic mingled with a hint of lavender, overlaid with lemon polish, a smell that had remained unchanged over the years.

As Penny entered, her heart sank. At the counter stood Cheryl Tate. She felt Fischer sneak behind her legs.

Cheryl had never been one for bothering about her appearance, but today she was more disheveled than usual. The greasy strands of her hair hung limply around her face, which bore the scowl that was permanently etched into her features. She grabbed the paper bag off the counter and turned quickly, not even thanking Mr Jones, the chemist, for his help, and bumped into Penny dropping the bag.

The collision was minor, but Cheryl's reaction was anything but. Her sharp retort was like a slap in the quiet pharmacy. "Can't you watch where you're going?" she snapped, her voice dripping with hatred and disdain. Penny, ever the peacemaker, bent down to help Cheryl pick up the fallen items, her actions a silent rebuttal to Cheryl's rudeness. Not that Cheryl would notice. She picked up the box of sleeping pills and extended it towards Cheryl, her concern for Gary momentarily overshadowing Cheryl's harsh demeanor.

"I hope Gary feels better soon," Penny said, her voice carrying a genuine concern. She'd seen Gary's name on the prescription label. Cheryl snatched the box from Penny's hand, her eyes shooting daggers.

"That's none of your business," she spat out before storming out of the pharmacy, leaving a cold trail of bitterness in her wake.

Penny stared after her. Gary must be bad if Cheryl was running errands for him. She made a mental note to go and see him as soon as she had some spare time.

"Good afternoon, Penny. Hello there, Fischer," Mr Jones said, after a brief disapproving frown at his departing customer. "I have your tablets here." He reached under the counter and gave Penny a paper bag.

"Thanks, Mr Jones."

"Fischer's just missed his friends. Daisy and Gatsby were in not more than half an hour ago."

"For the same reason, I assume? It's such a shame I have to give tablets to Fischer. I'd rather not give him anything, but he's too afraid of the loud bangs."

"I have two rescues of my own, you know, and they're the same," Mr Jones said. "Although Albert is better than he was. He's becoming deaf in his old age, so I expect that's the reason."

"You would have thought someone would have invented an alternative by now."

Mr. Jones adjusted his glasses and leaned slightly over the counter, his face lighting up with a hint of enthusiasm.

"It's funny you mention that, Penny. There's a town in Italy that took a significant step towards reducing the noise pollution caused by fireworks. They passed a local ordinance mandating the use of quieter fireworks to lessen the stress on animals, both domestic and wild."

Penny was immediately interested. "Really? I've never heard of it."

"Oh, indeed," Mr. Jones continued, "They aren't completely silent, but are designed to produce less noise compared to traditional fireworks. They lack the big aerial explosions that are usually associated with fireworks displays."

"That sounds intriguing. So, how do they work?" Penny asked, genuinely curious.

Mr. Jones smiled, "Well, these quieter fireworks utilise ex-

isting non-loud forms of fireworks. For instance, there are ef-
fects like the 'comet tail' that shoots into the sky with a trail of
sparkles before quietly fizzling out."

"Oh, yes, I remember mum and dad using those when I
was young. And I always had sparklers. They were quiet."

"It's the same concept. More about the visual effect than
the decibel levels. Which aren't necessary in my opinion. Se-
lecting to use these quieter types creates a fabulous display but
is less disturbing to animals and people who are sensitive to
loud noises."

Penny appreciated the insight. "It sounds like a perfect alternative. It's a shame they aren't more common here,
especially considering the distress loud fireworks cause to animals like Fischer."

Mr. Jones agreed, "Absolutely. And it's not just about
comfort, it's about inclusivity. Quieter fireworks allow more
people and animals to participate in celebrations without fear
or discomfort. I do hope as awareness grows, we'll see a shift
towards adopting such considerate alternatives."

"I do too, Mr Jones."

Penny thanked the pharmacist and stepped out of the
shop, the thought of quiet firework displays lingering in her
mind. No doubt it hadn't caught on nationwide, or world-
wide for that matter, due to the cost. The technology sounded
complicated. She'd do a bit of research in the future to see
what she could come up with. Christmas and New Year were
round the corner and there were always fireworks then.
Wouldn't it be wonderful if they could have quiet displays in
the villages?

———— ● ————

She didn't know it, but Penny was in for a bit of a shock when she got to the main library.

She parked the van in the car-park across the street and she and Fischer waited to cross the road before bounding up the steps.

Inside, Sam and Emma were busy checking out books for some patrons. The children's reading room was empty. It looked like the storyteller had gone for the day. A moment later, with the customers gone, Penny went to greet her colleagues.

They exchanged pleasantries and a bit of town gossip. Emma mentioned the upcoming bonfire and firework display, and Sam shared a funny anecdote about a recent encounter with a quirky patron.

Sam chuckled as he began, "You won't believe what happened earlier this week, Penny. We had the eccentric Mr. Higgins in."

"The one with the wild, untamed beard and a penchant for medieval history?"

Sam nodded. "That's him. Well, he came in on Tuesday, bustling with excitement. He told me he had finally traced his lineage back to a knight who served under King Edward III. He was so thrilled about it that he decided to pay homage in a rather... unconventional way."

Penny leaned in, already amused by the image of Mr. Higgins she had in her mind.

Sam continued, "The next day, Mr. Higgins walks into the library wearing a full knight's armor! Can you believe it? He was clanking around the library, sounding like a rock concert in a pot and pan shop staged by five-year-olds. The sight was absolutely surreal. He approached the medieval history section with a sense of purpose, as if he was on a quest for the Holy Grail or something."

Penny burst into laughter, imagining the scene.

"But that's not all," Sam added, trying to contain his own laughter. "He insisted on referring to Emma and me as his 'noble squires' and asked us to help him 'vanquish the dragon of ignorance' by finding more books on medieval warfare. The other patrons didn't know whether to be amused or scared. It was a scene straight out of a Monty Python sketch!"

Penny was laughing heartily now. "Oh, I wish I'd been here to witness Sir Higgins in action!"

Suddenly, there was silence and Penny saw Emma and Sam exchange a look.

"What?" Penny asked. "What is it?"

"We have a surprise for you," Emma said. "Well, actually it's for Fischer."

The little dog looked up and cocked his head to the side at the sound of his name.

Penny rounded the counter and found underneath a brand new bed for her little dog. But it wasn't just an ordinary bed, it was the most exquisite replica of her own cottage in Cherrytree Downs. The doorway was a cutout, perfect size for a Jack Russell, and after an excited sniff all the way around the miniature building, Fischer settled inside on his new cushion and let out a groan of utter contentment.

"Wow," she said, her eyes widening with delight. "This is beautiful. Wherever did it come from?"

"Henri Shattock built it," Sam said. "Brilliant isn't it?"

Emma chimed in, "You know she's been helping build the new shelving in the reference section? She finished much faster than we expected. She's done a fantastic job there as well. Anyway, this was made from the off-cuts."

Penny knelt down to get a closer look at the miniature cottage. The attention to detail was astonishing. The little windows were adorned with tiny curtains, and there was even a minuscule flower box under each window, filled with petite, artificial flowers. She could see the craftsmanship that went into creating this charming little abode for Fischer. It was a piece of art.

"It's certainly got Fischer's seal of approval," Penny said, smiling indulgently at her little pal, who was now cosily nestled inside the cottage, his eyes slowly closing. "This is just... I'm lost for words."

Sam chuckled. "Henri said she enjoyed every bit of crafting it. She even painted it to match the color of your actual cottage."

Penny stood up, still admiring the dog bed. "I must thank her personally. This is beyond thoughtful. And look at Fischer, he's already making himself at home."

Emma grinned. "It's a housewarming gift, library style!"

Penny laughed, the warmth of the gesture making her a bit emotional. "Right, I better get on with emptying the van. Won't be long." She said, tearing her eyes away from the adorable scene of Fischer snoozing in his new little home. One paw over his snout.

She was in the car-park at her van, juggling a box of books, when she felt a presence behind her.

"Hello, Penny."

"Edward. Hello. How are you?

"Fine thanks. Here, let me get that for you," he said, taking the box. "How are you getting on? Everything okay with work?"

Penny opened her mouth to answer, but words failed her. How are you? How's work? Offering to carry the heavy book box? This was absolutely not the Edward she knew. In fact, the only time he had ever commented on her job was to belittle or ridicule it. And she couldn't even remember the last time he asked her how she was. He'd never had much of a sense of humour, but he sounded downright morose at the moment.

"Yes, all well, thanks. So, you're all right, are you?"

"Oh fine," he replied. But he sounded downbeat. "How are your parents' doing? I haven't seen them for a while. I usually bump into them around town from time to time. Are they keeping okay?"

Now Penny really needed to sit down. She sat on the bumper of the van and looked up at Edward. Scrutinising his face for any clue as to what was going on. There was no hint of insincerity. He genuinely was interested in how her mum and dad were.

"They're both well. I'll tell them you were asking after them."

Edward was peering inside the van and Penny thought, oh here it comes, some barbed comment about the pointlessness of the mobile library service.

"Is Fish Face not with you today?"

Her mouth dropped open and Penny realised she had a face like a fish herself.

"He's inside the library with Emma and Sam. Edward, what's going on?"

"I'm getting married," he blurted out. "In the summer."

"Oh, congratulations."

Edward shrugged, but before Penny could analyse his response, he looked up and recoiled at what he saw. Richard Sole marching towards them, fists clenched at his sides and a murderous look on his face.

"Just what the heck are you playing at?" he shouted at Edward. "You're out here having a nice little chat while we're supposed to be having a meeting. I've been waiting at your office for half an hour!"

"Actually, Mr Sole, I think you'll find our meeting is scheduled for tomorrow, Friday. This happens to be my lunch break. Later than normal because I've been working on your portfolio. But rest assured, I'll have all the figures, feedback and advice you'll need tomorrow."

Sole waved his hand dismissively. "Just get that money working for me. Stop hanging around on the street. If I don't see some progress tomorrow, I'll be taking my money elsewhere."

Richard Sole walked towards his car, parked a couple of rows up from Penny's van. The bright red sports car engine roared into life and Sole pulled out, lowering the window and leering at them both.

"You really ought to get that repaired," Penny said, unable to resist taking a dig at the horrible man, pointing at the broken light.

Suddenly he braked, pulled on the handbrake and got out

of the car. Edward moved gallantly in front of her, but Sole swerved past him.

"Listen, my dear. What you know about cars I bet you could write on the back of a postage stamp and still leave space for your shopping list. Why don't you stick to books? I'm all for you having a little job while you wait to get married, but leave man's things alone. You'll just confuse your mind with stuff you don't understand." He turned and jabbed a finger in Edward's face. "Tomorrow."

"What a horrible, horrible man," Penny said, as Sole shot out of the car park with a squeal of tyres. "I don't know how you can remain civil to him, Edward."

"He's a client. It goes with the job, unfortunately."

"And talking of jobs, I really need to get back to work."

"Yes, me too. I'll carry your boxes to the door for you."

"Thanks, Edward."

NINE

Back in the main library, with all the books put away, and the van filled with those she needed for the following week, Penny was in the kitchen making tea. The rhythmic clinking of the spoon against the cup was a familiar sound that usually brought her comfort, but today it seemed to be setting her teeth on edge. Mind you, it was hardly surprising. A lot had happened since the previous Saturday.

The door swung open, revealing Emma, her face carrying a mix of excitement and seriousness that immediately caught Penny's attention.

"Emma, you look like you've just discovered a first edition, Dickens," Penny joked, trying to lighten the mood, though her heart raced with a mix of anticipation and concern. She knew something was up.

Emma's hands trembled slightly as she held out a brown envelope, the stamp of The British Library boldly embossed on the front. The significance of the envelope hit Penny like a ton of bricks.

"Oh my goodness, Emma...is this...?" Penny's voice trailed off, her eyes widening as Emma nodded.

Penny knew that Emma had always hankered after a research position at the British library. Ever since Emma had shared stories of her grandmother, who had been a librarian in London during the war, protecting invaluable manuscripts from the clutches of destruction during the Blitz, she had dreamed of being part of a place that housed history within its walls. But vacancies were like hen's teeth and the competition when a position did come up was fierce.

"I've been offered it, yes, but I haven't formally accepted yet. I wanted to talk to you first."

"But that's brilliant, Emma. Well done and huge congratulations. You really deserve it. But how I can help? Is there something stopping you from saying yes?"

"Crikey no. I'll definitely accept. It's a dream come true. It won't start until the new year, though."

"Then what is it?"

"Well, obviously, I'll need to be replaced. Sam isn't interested in becoming the branch manager. His goal is to have his own bookshop in a quirky little back street in London ever since he watched Hugh Grant in Notting Hill. But, to be perfectly honest, Penny, you're the best person for the job."

"Me?" Penny said. "But I have a job. I'm the county mobile librarian."

Penny had always cherished the mobile library service, a brainchild of hers birthed from a blend of love for books, inherited and instilled in her by her parents who had originally owned a bookshop in Winstoke before retiring, and a deep-seated commitment to community service. It was more than just a job for her; it was a mission, a tangible extension of her belief in the power of literature to bridge gaps, both geographical and generational.

The inception of the mobile library was a proud moment in her life. She had meticulously put together a business proposal, outlining the potential impact and the logistical framework of the service, and after rounds of meetings and revisions, it was accepted. It was a victory not just for her, but for every individual in the county villages whose access to the world of books was limited. And not just books. One particularly bad winter, she'd used the van to deliver food parcels to those who'd been snowed in.

As she stood there, contemplating the prospect of leaving her beloved mobile library, her heart ached at the thought of parting from something that was an integral part of her identity, something that meant the world to her. Who was she if not the mobile librarian?

"I know, and you're brilliant at it," Emma said. "But you know this library system just as well, if not better than me. The patrons all know and like you, and it is a much better salary."

"Are you going to appeal to my sense of civic duty next?" Penny asked with a smile.

"No, of course not," Emma said, laughing. "I'd just like to know this place is in good hands when I go. It's been a part of my life for so long. I'll really miss being here. It's like leaving home all over again. But this is the job I've been working towards," she said, shaking the envelope.

"Is it London or Yorkshire?"

"Yorkshire. I have family up there."

Penny briefly put her head in her hands. "But what about my regular customers? You know how important the mobile service is for the villages. Most of them are old and can't travel to town. It's a social hub for them."

"Actually, Henri is very keen to become the mobile librarian if you decide to take over here."

"Hello? Is anyone making the tea? A man could die of thirst out here."

"Sorry, Sam, it's almost done. Emma was just bringing me up to date with her news. I'll finish the tea and we can go back through and chat more there. Fischer is on his own."

"I'm going back now," Sam said. "Don't worry, Fischer is still fast asleep in his own personal mansion."

Back in the main library over tea, Emma and Sam told Penny about Henri Shattock.

She'd taken to the library systems like the proverbial duck to water apparently and had loved every minute of it. Emma had called her an exceptionally quick study and the brightest of sparks.

"She was here when I received the job offer," Emma said. "And asked if there would be a job vacancy and how could she apply?"

Penny smiled. "She wanted the manager position?"

"No. She's sensible enough to know she's nowhere near ready for that. But she did suggest you."

"Which meant she'd be able to take over the mobile library?"

"Got it in one," Sam said. "But that wasn't the only reason. She genuinely thinks you'd be the best to take over from Emma, Penny. She knows and likes you, so if she does take on the mobile service, she said she couldn't think of a better person to have as a boss."

"That's very kind of her. And she was instrumental in getting my van fixed up so..."

"Oh, she won't need your van. Penny, if that's what you're thinking?" Emma said. "That's yours. She actually has an old horse box she keeps at the riding stables. She said that would be perfect once she'd done it up."

Penny sighed and looked away, sipping her tea. This had all come out of the blue and she felt as though decisions about her life and her job were being made for her. Then again, the additional money would come in very useful. It was true that while she loved her job, there was very little of her wage left at the end of every month.

Emma put a hand on her shoulder. "We don't want you to feel as though you're being railroaded, Penny. You can absolutely say no and continue as you are. We'll start the interview process and find someone else to take over from me. We just thought you'd like to be given first option, that's all."

"And if you do take over from Em and Henri takes over from you, there's no reason why you can't do a swapsie on some days, is there?" Sam said. "One day a week or something. That way, you'll still be out and about seeing your regulars and I can help Henri when she's here."

For the first time since she'd heard the news, Penny felt

the load lighten. Could she actually have the best of both worlds?

"That's a great idea, Sam," Emma said. "Now why didn't I think of that? But let's not get ahead of ourselves. I'm sorry, Penny, I feel as if we've ambushed you."

"Don't worry. I'll need time to think it all through, though."

"Of course you will. So, to change the subject completely, I saw you talking with Edward earlier."

"Did you? Yes, he came to tell me he's getting married."

"Wow, really? Are you okay with that?"

"Absolutely. Edward and I are ancient history. I'm pleased for him."

"I saw that awful Richard Sole character join you. I'm surprised he hasn't got his fancy red car fixed since Trevor Smith reversed into it."

"Or bought a new one," Sam said. "I've never seen anyone flash his cash so obviously as that man does. He's the sort of bloke who'd get a new car just because the ash tray is full."

"Wait," Penny said to Emma. "You saw Trevor hit Richard's car? When was this?"

"Monday morning. In the car-park across the street. He reversed right into it, then drove off. I opened up and came in and wrote a note to leave on Richard's car about what I'd seen, but when I got out there, both he and his car were gone. I meant to tell him when I saw him next. But what with the job offer and being busy here, it slipped my mind. Is it important?"

Penny shook her. "I'm not sure. But I need to tell John."

"Yes, it's time to close now, anyway."

"See you at the bonfire later?" Penny asked.

"Yes, we'll be there. Bye, Penny. Bye, Fischer."

———— ● ————

It was Fischer who spied John Monroe first. He was across the street talking on his phone, head down. He looked up and gave her a wave as Fischer barked in recognition.

She skipped down the steps and, after waiting for a couple of cars to pass, jogged across the road to greet him.

"Hi. Were you waiting for me?"

"I was," he said, pulling her in for a kiss, after greeting an enthusiastic little dog. "I finished work early for a change, but was just trying to arrange for someone to pick up an abandoned car. It's been left in the country lane about ten miles from here. It belongs to Gary Tait."

"Maybe it's run out of petrol? Have you tried phoning Thatchings?"

"Yes, but there's no answer. I don't suppose you have a mobile number for him, do you?"

Penny shook her head. "I'm sorry I don't."

"That's a pity. If he or his wife can't collect it in an hour, it will have to be towed away. I'd like to save him that fee if I can."

"That's thoughtful of you."

"All in a day's work for a humble copper," he said with a grin. "It's not all chasing bank robbers, you know."

"When was the last time you chased a bank robber?"

Monroe shrugged. "It was a few years ago, back when I was a lowly constable pounding the streets. I got him, but it was a sad case. A last resort for a man who'd lost his job and couldn't afford to feed his family. But enough of that. What news have you got since we last spoke?"

They began to walk back over to Penny's van, hand in hand.

"Well, that certainly put me in my place." Penny said. "Actually, I have quite a lot of news. Do have time for a cup of tea in the van and I'll tell you about it?"

Over steaming mugs, sat on the camping chairs, Penny brought John up to date with her news. Starting with Edward's impending marriage and the subsequent dressing down he'd had when Richard Sole turned up. She then told him what Emma said about Trevor Smith reversing into Sole's red sports car and driving off. It was at this point John put down his tea and began making notes.

"Well, Sole hasn't reported the damage," John said. "I would have known."

"He strikes me as the sort of person who would deal with that sort of thing privately," Penny said, and John agreed.

"And the final news. Emma has secured a senior research position at The British Library in Yorkshire. She wants me to take over in Winstoke as branch manager."

"A big move. How do you feel about it? I've no doubt you'll be able to do the job with your eyes closed, but it depends on whether you'll be happy to give up the mobile library. The villagers will certainly miss you. When do they need to know by?"

"I've got a bit of leeway. She wouldn't start her job until the New Year. I'm thinking about it. It's actually a promotion and Sam had a really good idea. Apparently Henri Shattock would love my current job. She has an old horse box she's dying to make into a library. Sam's suggestion was that one day a week we'd swap places. A different day and, therefore, a different village each week. So I'd still be able to keep in touch with the village regulars."

"I can just see Henri doing that," John grinned. "And Sam's idea seems like a good solution. Sorry, hang on, that's my phone."

He opened the door and stepped out into the bitter air, closing the door behind him. Penny cleared up the tea things and put away the chairs while she waited. She stepped out when she saw him end the call.

"Sorry about that. I've got to go. So much for finishing early. Listen, whatever you decide about the job, I'll support you one-hundred per cent. You know that."

"Thank you, John. Are you at the bonfire tonight?"

"I am. In a semi-official capacity. I'll see you there."

Penny waved him off, then got in the van. It was time to go home.

TEN

To Penny's dismay, she could already hear distant fireworks exploding in the distance by the time she and Fischer exited the van outside her house. They seemed to get earlier and earlier every year. Inside, she wrapped one of the sedatives in a hunk of cheese and threw it in the air for her little dog. He caught it and wolfed it down, then looked at her reproachfully. Penny shook her head in amazement. Even disguised in his favourite treat, he knew what she'd done.

With the bangs and whizzes outside getting louder, Fischer crawled under the kitchen table.

"It's okay, little man," she said, crawling in with him, stroking his head, and sent a text to her mum asking if she'd come now to pick Fischer up in the car. It would be too frightening for him to walk. She got a positive response a moment later.

Then there was an almighty roar that caused both Penny and Fischer to jump. A huge rocket raced upward and exploded in a deafening crack. It lit the sky with a bloom of sparkling fire that illuminated the kitchen in all colours of the rainbow.

Penny swore as Fischer shivered in her arms and hoped her mum would turn up soon. A couple of minutes later, the front door opened and closed and her mum trotted up the hall into the kitchen.

"Hello, love. How is he? Oh, you poor little man. Come on sweetie, let's get you in the car and home with me," Sheila Finch said, scooping Fischer into her arms.

"Thanks mum. He's just had a sedative, so it should begin to work soon."

"It's that stupid man, Richard Sole. He must be burning through hundreds of pounds out there. No thought for anyone else, or the animals that will be terrified. In my opinion, they should ban the sale of personal fireworks and have organised legitimate displays only. You can hardly see a foot in front of your face due to all the smoke. And goodness knows where they'll all land when they come down. It's irresponsible. There's thatched roofs in this village. You'd have thought he'd know the risk with him living in one. The man's an idiot."

"I agree, mum. It breaks my heart to see Fischer so petrified. Thanks for looking after him."

"There's nothing me and your father like more, Penny. We've seen the annual bonfire display so many times. We'd much rather be looking after Fish Face. I'd better go while there's a bit of a lull outside. Fingers crossed, I can get us both home and in the house before he starts up again. Have a good time, love."

After she'd waved her mum and Fischer off, Penny ran up-stairs to change into jeans and a warm jumper. Downstairs, she shrugged into her big coat and felt something in the deep pocket. It was the strip of cloth Fischer had found attached to the old furniture shop window. She stuffed it back into her pocket. She'd put it in a bin later.

Bonfire night was the last village event in the season before Christmas and clearly all those who lived in the area, barring the elderly, or those who were pet sitting like her parents, had turned out for the occasion. There seemed to be a fair few tourists as well. The designated car park at one side of the field was full, so Penny parked on the roadside, like many others had, and walked the rest of the way. The hedgerows surrounding the field had been adorned with twinkling fairy lights in red, green, and white, which added to the festive atmosphere. They were new, and Penny thought they looked great.

She surveyed the crowd, wondering how on earth she was going to find John, Susie, and the children. She decided to walk the perimeter first. The vendors were once again out in force and doing a roaring trade. Candy floss and toffee apples were big draws and Penny, in the spirit of the occasion, de-cided a toffee apple was just the thing. She hadn't had one for years and had forgotten how good they tasted. Linda Green had brought her mobile kitchen to the field and was serving hot drinks, burgers, and bacon sandwiches.

Old Fred was once again on the tannoy announcing the fire lighting time and when the firework display would start. They were peppered with safety broadcasts and advertise-ments for local shops and services.

Penny eventually spotted Susie and the kids buying hot

chocolate and was making a beeline for her when she narrowly missed being bumped into by Trevor Smith. She got out of the way just in time, but the woman behind her wasn't so lucky. He bounced off her, causing her to falter and drop the food she'd been holding. He strode on, not even bothering to apologise. He was taking small sips from a pop bottle as he walked.

Somewhere in the crowd, a voice boomed out. Instantly recognisable as Harry Slade, arguing with someone as he aggressively held his spot at the front of the tape cordon surrounding the bonfire. Penny shook her head. Slade was always arguing with someone. This time he was saying he had a right to be here because this was his pitch. The place where he stood when fielding the cricket team. It was nonsense, of course. The turf was stripped for the fire and replaced afterwards so there was no damage. He was just spoiling for a fight. Penny realised that the promotion match was to have been played earlier and guessed they'd had to forfeit the match, otherwise they'd still be on the bus. No wonder he was so furious.

She moved on, trying to catch a glimpse of Susie. She and the children had moved on from where she'd last seen them and were once again lost in the crowd. She sauntered the length of the barrier, craning her neck over the crowd as she went. A man dipped under the tape wearing a hi vis jacket and walked towards the team preparing to light the fire. No doubt a fire marshal. Penny couldn't hear the conversation, but from the gestures, the man was being asked to step away. He didn't. Hands on his hips, he shook his head and gesticulated wildly towards the bonfire, the crowd, and then the men themselves. Eventually, after what could only have been a diplomatic response from the real team leader, the man turned and walked away. It was Richard Sole. No doubt attempting to buy the right to start the fire. He might have enough money to buy half the village, but the man clearly felt his wealth gave him the right to get his own way in everything. He must have set off driving here at the same time Penny was getting changed. That meant her mum would have got Fischer home safely without any more fireworks from Sole, which was a huge relief.

She was still glancing at the crowd when she finally spotted John talking to a couple of uniformed officers. She changed direction and, as if some sixth sense had told him she was there, he turned. His face breaking out into a huge smile. He walked to meet her, leaving the constables to move into the crowd.

"Hi. I was wondering where you were," he said, bending to give her a kiss. "You taste of toffee apples. Reminds me of my youth." Penny raised an eyebrow, mirth dancing in her eyes. John grinned. "That sounded better in my head. But you know what I mean."

Penny nodded. "I do. I've been thinking about Martin's murder, John. Do you have time for a chat?"

"Of course. But let's go somewhere we can't be overheard."

They bought tea from a vendor and sat at a bench on the outskirts of the field next to the hedgerow.

"Have you got the forensic results back from Trevor and Richard's cars?" Penny asked.

"The preliminary report, yes. There are still a couple of tests to do, but it looks like the only damage was caused by one hitting the other. There's nothing to suggest either of them hit Martin. It looks like you were right, Penny. Although heaven knows where this leaves the investigation."

"I've had a thought about that."

"Go on."

"We've been concentrating on three potential suspects," John smirked at the word 'we', however Penny plowed on. "But so far, we have nothing that puts any of them at the scene. I know they all argued with Martin the night of the Halloween party. There were witnesses to all of them. You and me included. But what if it wasn't any of them, John? What if the person who killed Martin is someone we haven't thought of?"

John looked into the distance, a frown on his face, while he stirred his tea and thought about her suggestion.

"Okay," he said eventually. "Let's assume you're right. What about motive? Martin had threatened to report Trevor for drink driving. Harry Slade needed the team bus fixed to move up the cricket league and was making considerable money from match fixing. That's being investigated by another department, by the way. But Martin had deemed the bus unroadworthy and refused to work on it any further. Then there's Richard Sole, who wanted Martin's garage. All of those are motives in my book. So who else would have a reason to kill Martin? And what could it be? We've been investigating this non stop since Martin was found, yet we've come up with nothing that even resembles a lead that would point to someone else being the killer, Penny."

"But, by the same token, you haven't been able to prove it was any of those three men either."

John nodded. "True. So what do you suggest?"

"This is the last county celebration before Christmas. All

the villagers who can travel are here. But, more to the point, it's probable that the same people who were at the Halloween event are also here. Maybe it's time to appeal to the public. What about using the tannoy system to appeal for witnesses? Someone must have seen something, John, even if they didn't recognise it for what it was at the time."

John smiled. Putting his arm around her shoulder, he drew her in closer and kissed the top of her head. Resting his chin on her hair as he spoke.

"That's a good idea, Penny. I'll do that now. I think I see Susie and the children coming over."

Penny looked up and waved. "I've been looking all over for them."

"Okay, I'll see you shortly."

Susie and the kids were wheeling their guy over to the bonfire when she caught up with them.

"Hey, you two. Ready to put your guy on the fire? How has the collection been going? I haven't forgotten I promised you a bit more. Here you are," Penny said, handing them a five-pound note. "Don't burn it."

"We won't. Thank you, Aunt Penny. We've made a hundred pounds."

"That's amazing. Well done." Penny turned to Susie. "Just the three of you tonight?"

"Ever the detective. It's great to have them back."

There was a double chime that echoed around the field, and Monroe's voice came over the microphone.

"Ladies and gentleman, may I have your attention please? This is Detective Inspector John Monroe from Winstoke police station. I'm reaching out for your assistance regarding a serious incident that occurred during the recent Halloween event. That evening, a fatal assault took place and a member of our community lost his life. Given the nature of this crime, I believe some of you may have witnessed the incident or have valuable information that could assist the investigation. I understand this is an unexpected request during this evening's celebration, but your cooperation is crucial. If you were in the vicinity of the cemetery just outside Thistle Grange at the time or noticed anything unusual, please approach one of the officers present tonight, or call the Winstoke station. Every piece of information, no matter how small, can help. Thank you for your cooperation. I'll now hand back to Fred."

Susie turned back to Penny with a questioning look.

Penny shook her head in reply, aware of two pairs of little ears listening to every word.

"Right then, kids," Susie said. "Shall we take your guy over to the fire marshal?"

The kids followed their mum, Billy pulling the cart with Ellen at his side carrying the collection tin. Penny brought up the rear. From her vantage point, she had a good view of the dummy and once again she noticed the shirt. Suddenly, she stopped.

"Wait!"

Susie and the children turned round.

"What's the matter, Penny?" Susie asked, concern etched on her face. "Are you all right?"

"I'm fine. Susie, where did you get this shirt? The kids said you gave it to them."

"Tom found it. I told you he was renting in Hambleton Chase. He saw a woman putting it into the recycling bin, so retrieved it for me once she'd gone. He knew I was looking for something for the guy. I think he wanted to help them make it, actually." She suddenly looked down at the quizzical look on her daughter's face.

"Who's Tom, mummy?" Ellen said.

"Just someone I work with, sweetie. Penny, what is it?"

Penny whisked the scrap of cloth from her coat pocket and held it next to the torn shirt. It was a perfect match. Suddenly, she knew exactly what had happened.

"Sorry, I have to go and speak to John.

"You've solved it then?"

Penny nodded. "Yes, I think I have. Don't burn the guy until I get back. I need the shirt."

ELEVEN

Penny ran through the crowd to the last place she knew he'd been. At the tannoy system with Fred. But he was no longer there.

"Fred, I need to speak to John Monroe. Could you announce over the system for him to come back here, please?"

"Of course I can, Penny. You wait there. No doubt he'll be along shortly after."

Penny stamped her feet while she waited. It seemed an age until John turned up.

"I know that look, Penny. What have you found out?"

They'd moved to the rear of the tent where Fred had set up out of the noise and crowds.

"I know who killed Martin, John. Cheryl Tait."

"It can't be Cheryl, Penny. She has an alibi. I've interviewed her myself and there are half a dozen people who saw her at their pop up shop in the old furniture place."

"Yes, she was there, but not all night. She and Gary had a

massive row and Gary stormed off. Cheryl disappeared inside. It was really embarrassing to witness. I assumed she'd gone to lick her wounds in private. I never saw her again."

"But you'd moved on too. She could have come out after you'd left."

Penny shook her head.

"I was walking Fischer round the back of the shop on Wednesday and he found a scrap of material stuck on the window latch. I took it and closed the window. I'd forgotten all about it, but I still have it. Look." She thrust the torn piece of fabric in his hand.

"But what does this prove?"

"It belongs to the shirt Cheryl was wearing that night. Susie's kids have the rest of it on their guy. It's a match, John, I've checked. And Tom saw a woman putting the ruined shirt in the recycling. He pulled it out, as he knew Susie was looking for one. I'm sure he'd be able to identify Cheryl if asked. Like I said, she went inside the furniture shop after her row with Gary, but then climbed out of the window, ripping her shirt in the process. She then got in her car and ran Martin down."

"But why would she do that? It doesn't make any sense. She and Martin didn't know one another that well, did they? What would she have to gain?"

"She didn't mean to kill Martin. It was an accident. She thought it was Gary."

"So you're saying she was really trying to kill her husband and mistook Martin for him?"

"Exactly!" Penny snapped her fingers. "Gary told me when he got back that night Cheryl looked shocked. Well, she would if she already thought she'd killed him. Both Gary and Martin were wearing the same costume, and in the dark, it would be easy to make that mistake."

"Look, I'm not saying you're wrong, but Martin would have literally been a dead weight. How would she have managed to drag him from the road and into the graveyard on her own?"

"Adrenaline, for one thing. It's known that in a heightened state of shock, people are capable of incredible feats of strength. Desperation is another. Besides, Cheryl isn't as weak as you think. Running Thatchings involves a lot of strength. Who do you think changes the beer barrels?"

"Why would she want to kill Gary?" Monroe was becoming increasingly concerned.

"Because he wanted a divorce. That's what the row was about. It was the last thing he said. Everyone heard him."

"There are easier ways to try and work things out than resort to murder, Penny. Couldn't they have tried counselling?"

"Gary was adamant. But that's not the issue. Thatchings is still in Gary's parents' name. He and Cheryl are purely employees. If they divorced, she'd be entitled to nothing. She wants the business. What happened to the car, by the way?"

"Car?"

"The Tait's car. You said it had been abandoned, and you were arranging to tow it."

John's eyes widened. "It was burning when they arrived, apparently. They had to get the fire brigade out there to make it safe."

"Well, didn't anyone go and visit the Taits to find out what happened?"

There must have been something in Penny's tone as John bristled at the implication he hadn't done his job properly.

"Sorry," she said.

"A PC went round and informed them both. As far as I am aware, and remember, this wasn't my case. I was just trying to save them the aggravation of having their car towed. Cheryl said she'd run out of petrol and had walked home to tell Gary what had happened. The subsequent damage was put down to local hooligans."

"She was getting rid of the evidence."

John nodded grimly. "In hindsight, that could be the case."

"Oh no!" Penny felt an ice cold shiver run down her spine. She gripped hold of John's arm. "Gary's in danger. I think she means to kill him. I saw her buying sleeping pills at the pharmacy. She needs to get rid of him or she won't inherit the business when his parents die. Come on, we need to get over there."

Penny grabbed his arm and dragged him towards the gate.

"Penny, where are you going?"

"To my van. It's just on the road."

"We could have used my car, you know," he replied, jogging beside her.

"Where is it?" Penny asked, unlocking the library and jumping in. John got in the passenger side and put on his belt before answering.

"In the car park."

"It would take too long to get it out." She revved the engine and, after checking for on-coming vehicles, pulled out onto the country lane.

"I can't believe I didn't see it sooner," Penny said, slowing for a tight bend. The road narrowed considerably here, high hedgerows closing in on both sides. The foliage looked supernatural and foreboding in the narrow headlights of the van. "I've never been a fan of Cheryl and I know the feeling is mutual, but I never thought she'd be capable of anything like this."

"Don't blame yourself, Penny. Believe me, I'm just as annoyed with myself. But the starting point of any suspicious death or murder investigation is always the victim. Did they have enemies? Was there anyone with a perceived grudge against them? Never, ever, do the police start with the assumption of mistaken identity. It just isn't feasible."

"No, you're right. It would make it impossible. But I'll never forgive myself if something happens to Gary."

Even though she controlled the vehicle like a professional, Penny was driven by an urgency to get to Thatchings as quickly as possible and exceeded the speed limit. Gary's life might well depend on it.

TWELVE

Thatchings was eerily silent when they arrived. The gravel drive, normally filled with resident's cars, was clear and crunched audibly under their feet as they approached the heavy oak door.

Monroe hammered on the wood, but there was no reply. Penny tried the handle. Locked.

"I'm going round the back," she said.

Using the torch function on her phone, Penny rounded the side of the old building, shining the light into darkened windows. The furniture cast spooky shadows on the walls, and Penny shuddered in response.

At the rear of the property, Penny's light found the kitchen. Equipped to cater for a dozen guests, it was a hybrid of old country and functional commercial.

The pine table was set for two, but there was only one chair. She spotted a full glass of wine next to one plate, but the second glass lay shattered on the flagstones. A few drops of the beverage looked black in the light of her torch.

"John," she called. "Over here."

John cupped his hands over his eyes and peered inside.

"There's something definitely wrong here." He turned. "What's that building at the end?"

He pointed to the small, modern bungalow. It was as dark as the main house.

"Gary's parents live there. They are really elderly and not in great health, John. I don't want to disturb them if we can help it."

At that moment, a firework shot up into the sky from the direction of Hambleton Chase. Exploding high overhead, it momentarily lit up the garden, and they saw two furrows ploughed through more gravel. Something had been dragged along here. Another explosion of light revealed a large garage, partially concealed behind a privet hedge.

"Come on, Penny."

John grabbed her hand, and they quickly followed the marks around a corner. They stopped in shock as they were met with a scene from a horror movie.

Later, Penny would tell Susie it felt as though she just stood there for ages, even though it was no more than a second. She took in the entire terrifying scene all at once, as though it imprinted on her brain in an instant. Everything came into sharp focus, the minutest of details clear.

Gary was sitting on a dining chair that had been lifted high up on a hydraulic jack. The sort of thing used to move catering equipment or car engines. He looked unconscious, and there was a noose around his neck. Penny followed the rope up and saw it had been looped over a dense beam.

Hands on the control of the jack, about to let it down and leave Gary swinging in midair was Cheryl.

Penny launched herself at the woman and grabbed her in a tackle any rugby player would be proud of. But she was too late. She heard the hiss of air escaping. The jack had lowered; the chair had fallen and Gary was dancing on the end of a rope.

Penny dived for his legs and lifted him up. He was making a terrifying choking noise, hands scrabbling at the rope tightening around his neck, cutting off his air supply. His eyes bulging.

"John! Help me, I can't hold him."

But John was already moving. Scrabbling up a wooden ladder, he'd leaned against the beam. Axe in hand.

"Brace yourself, Penny!" He yelled and chopped clean through the rope.

The sudden weight felled Penny, and she collapsed to the floor, winded, with Gary on top of her. She shifted position, desperately trying to get out from underneath. To remove the rope from Gary's neck and stop him from dying. But she couldn't move.

Suddenly, John was there. The rope was removed, flung to one side. He rolled Gary on his back, freeing Penny as he began CPR.

"Come on, Gary, stay with me!" he yelled.

Penny called for an ambulance and the police.

Suddenly Gary moved, then coughed. His eyes opened, and he stared at Penny for a moment before slumping back on the ground.

"It was Cheryl," he croaked. "Martin, the car damaged, set fire..." He began to cough.

"We know, Gary. We worked it all out," Penny said through tears, grasping his hand. "The ambulance is on its way. You're going to be fine."

An engine started on the drive, wheels spinning, throwing up gravel. Penny whirled round. Cheryl had gone.

"John. The library," she said in horror.

Monroe dashed off but was back a moment later, shaking his head. But was on his phone to the station requesting to be patched through immediately to all the cars in the area.

"All cars, I repeat, all cars. Stop the mobile library. Heading north from Thatchings. The driver is Cheryl Tait. She's heading towards the bypass. Arrest her immediately. The charge is murder."

The ambulance arrived swiftly, and Gary was loaded onto the stretcher. Penny held his hand all the way.

"Do you want me to come with you?" she asked.

Gary shook his head. "No. But, my parents."

"It's fine, Gary, I understand. I'll look after them and won't tell them what happened. Just that you've had a little fall and broken your wrist or something."

Gary nodded and closed his eyes. "Thanks, Penny."

John wandered over after finishing yet another call.

"They've caught her. She managed to get to the bypass, but one of our cars was blocking the slip road. She's in custody and on her way to the station. I'm on the way there now. Do you want to come?"

"Yes. Where's my van?"

"One of my officers is taking it back. He'll park it in your usual spot opposite the main library and leave the keys at the station."

"Thanks, John. Before we go, I need to check on Gary's parents. I promised him."

"I'll come with you. I'd like to check they're all right too. I'm surprised they haven't been woken up by everything going on out here."

"They won't have their hearing aids in. But I think there's a light just gone on, so someone is awake."

"There's a female officer arrived. If necessary, she can stay with them tonight. I'd feel happier if they weren't alone here."

Penny smiled and hugged him. "You're a good man, John Monroe."

THIRTEEN

Penny woke the next morning feeling groggy. She hadn't got back until nearly midnight. After sending a text from the police station to her mum explaining she'd pick Fischer up in the morning, she drove home and crawled into bed.

Luckily it was Friday, and she didn't have to go to work, but the house felt empty without her little pal and she was out of the door just after eight-thirty and on her parent's doorstep a few minutes later.

"Hello, love," Sheila Finch said, giving her daughter a hug. She was followed by a wiggling little dog who jumped into Penny's arms.

"Hi, mum. Hello, Fish Face." She hugged her little dog close for a moment, then popped him back on the floor. "How was he last night?" she asked her mum as they went through to the kitchen.

"As right as rain. Hardly bothered at all by the fireworks.

Sit yourself down. I'll get you some breakfast and you can tell us what happened last night."

"Hi, dad," she bent to give him a hug, stopping him momentarily reading the sports pages of the paper. Penny could see he was reading Susie's article about the match fixing.

"Hi, Penny. Have you seen this news? Well researched. Slade will lose his captaincy for sure now, I expect. It says there's a proper inquiry going on. Is that your John?"

Penny sat down and shook her head. "No, it's a different department. But it's pretty serious from what I can gather and goes beyond merely fixing matches. He's made a lot of money on the side."

Albert shook his head sadly. "In that case, he's likely to lose a lot more than his captaincy. It wouldn't have happened in my day. No one has any respect nowadays. It's all cutting corners and trying to make a fast buck, as our American friends say."

"Now," Sheila said, joining them after filling the table with tea and toast. "What happened last night? You look absolutely shattered, love, if you don't mind me saying so."

Albert neatly folded his paper, set it to one side, and gave Penny a concerned look.

"You caught them, didn't you? The person who killed Martin?"

Penny nodded. "It was Cheryl Tait."

For a split second, you could have heard a pin drop as both her parents stared at her, wide eyed and slack jawed. Then they both spoke at once.

"Cheryl Tait? But why? What on earth had Martin done to her?"

Penny waited until they both drew breath, then told them from the beginning what had happened and the reason. When she'd finished, Albert nodded briefly, then wandered silently out into the back garden, followed by Fischer, who sensed he was upset. Sheila was wiping her eyes on a tea towel.

"Oh, Penny. It's just awful. To think Martin was killed because she thought he was someone else. What a waste. And poor Gary. I know it's all very well saying it in hindsight, but he never should have married her. She's what your Gran would have called a wrong 'un. How is Gary, do you know?"

"Not yet. I'll call the hospital later. Or John, he'll probably know."

"You have a good one there, Penny. He saved Gary's life. I hope he gets an award or something."

"Me too, mum."

"Right," Albert said, marching back into the kitchen. Fischer hot on his heels. "Who wants coffee?"

The muted colors of November painted the landscape as Penny, and Fischer made their way up Sugar Hill. The once-green grass was now a tapestry of browns and golds, crunching softly underfoot. The trees in the distance had shed most of their leaves, standing tall and skeletal against the overcast sky. A chill hung in the air, a reminder that winter was just around the corner.

Fischer trotted alongside Penny, his breath visible in the cold. Now and then, he'd stop to investigate a rustling sound, perhaps a squirrel or a late bird foraging for food.

Reaching the summit, Penny felt the full force of the November wind. It whipped around her, making her pull her scarf tighter around her neck. From here, she could see the entirety of the village below, smoke rising from chimneys and people going about their day, bundled up against the chill.

She took a moment to appreciate the quiet beauty of it all, then her phone vibrated in her pocket, breaking her reverie. Seeing Susie's name on the screen, she answered, "Good morning, Susie."

"Hi, Penny. Where are you? You sound like you're in a wind tunnel."

Laughing lightly, Penny replied, "I'm on top of Sugar Hill. It's quite breezy up here. Fischer seems to be enjoying the cold more than I am. But at least it's waking me up."

"I should have guessed," Susie said. "Listen, I wanted to be the one to tell you before you heard it from anyone else. But Tom and I have broken up."

Penny's concern was evident in her voice. "Oh, Susie, I'm so sorry. What happened?"

"The age-old story. He's getting back with his ex. But, honestly, Penny, I'm absolutely fine about it." Susie's voice held a note of finality, and Penny could sense her friend's determination to move forward. "It was a whirlwind, really. Fun while it lasted, but not meant for the long haul. We're still on good terms, which is a relief since we work together. And he's been eying opportunities with the nationals. I think it's only a matter of time before he moves on."

Penny sighed, watching a flock of birds fly southward. "Life has its twists and turns, doesn't it? But you're strong,

Susie. There's someone out there for you, I know it. But in the meantime, have what fun you can."

Susie chuckled. "I intend to. And speaking of twists, I hear you and John had an eventful night."

Penny smiled, amused but not surprised the news had traveled so fast. It was par for the course when you lived in a village. She recounted the previous night's events, with Susie interrupting with questions. Ever the reporter, she could hear the scratching of her pen as she made notes.

By the end, Susie was full of praise. "You two never cease to amaze me. You really are great together. I'll visit Gary at the hospital later and send him your love. And now, if you'll excuse me, I have a front-page story to write. I promise, no typos in your name. Ciao for now."

Penny laughed, her breath forming little clouds in the cold air. "Stay warm, Susie."

She pocketed her phone and called Fischer, who had wandered off in search of a rabbit. The two of them began their descent, the village below beckoning them home.

At half-past five that evening, after a day spent cleaning, walking Fischer and watching another Agatha Christie film on television, Penny had received a call from John asking if she wanted to come over to his house that evening. The former police house had been newly refurbished with the help of Henri Shattock, and it would be the first time Penny had been allowed to see it. John had suggested a bottle of wine and a takeaway from the best Italian in Winstoke.

Two hours later, she was sitting at the kitchen table by can-dlelight, eating pasta surrounded by a beautiful bespoke oak kitchen. Henri had done an incredible job.

"Seems strange not having a little dog at our feet," John said, cutting into his lasagna.

"I know. But, he's having a wonderful time with mum and dad. I hear you've been to interview Gary. How is he?"

"In remarkably good form, considering. Still very croaky and bruised, but relieved, I think. His marriage had been going downhill for a while, from what I understand. I think he's glad it's over. His main concern was his parents. But they're fine. I have a family liaison officer with them for as long as they need."

"He made a full statement?"

John nodded. "We have everything needed to put Cheryl away for a long time. Including additional forensics from the car. It's been proved beyond a shadow of a doubt that it was used to knock Martin down, and that it was her who set fire to it. Fingerprints all over the can of petrol and we have her on CCTV at the garage where she bought it from. It was obvious what she was planning."

"Did Gary know what she'd done? He mentioned Martin and the car before he went into the ambulance."

"He worked it out. He'd seen the damage to their car and confronted Cheryl about it. A big mistake. She denied it, of course, but it set the wheels in motion for her to try to kill Gary sooner than she'd intended to."

"Yes, Gary mentioned to me that Cheryl had called a meeting for the two of them to try and patch things up. I'm glad we worked it out and got there in time, John. I can't bear to think..."

"Don't, Penny. You'll make yourself ill thinking like that. You solved it and we saved Gary's life. That's all there is to it." Penny smiled and nodded. "Anyway, in other news, Trevor Smith was finally caught driving under the influence. He's been banned from driving and his license confiscated. Apparently, there has also been a complaint that he tried to coerce a couple into giving him money for driving into his car when they were nowhere near it. So, you were right about that too. I doubt he'll ever be able to get behind a wheel again and it's possible he'll go to prison. Watch this space."

"That is really good news. And I have more. I saw a For Sale sign outside Richard Sole's house earlier. That's two trouble makers dealt with. So, about the third? What's happening with the investigation into Harry Slade?"

"It's not my case, as you know, but I had a chat with the DI running the operation and he's got enough to charge him. He made a serious amount of money betting on the outcomes of games he'd rigged. And it wasn't just cricket. Do you think perhaps we can dispense with the shoptalk now and spend some proper time together? I feel as though I haven't seen you for ages, Penny. More wine?"

Penny nodded and held out her glass. They spent the rest of the time enjoying their meal and talking about everything but the case.

An hour later, both wearing silly grins, they walked upstairs hand in hand.

Did you enjoy Out for the Count? It would be great if you could leave a review on the site where you bought it. It really helps other readers to find the books. Thank you.

*

FREE BOOK – The Yellow Cottage Mystery, the prequel short story to J. New's British historical mystery series, is yours as a thank you for joining her Reader's Group news-letter. You can find more information on the website: www.jnewwrites.com

*

Have you met Ella Bridges yet? England in the 1930s. **The Yellow Cottage Vintage Mysteries.** Immerse yourself in country house murders, dastardly deeds at English church fetes, daring escapades in the French Riviera and the secret tunnels under London, in the award-winning series readers call, 'Miss Marple' meets 'The Ghost Whisperer.'

THE BOOKS:
- An Accidental Murder
- The Curse of Arundel Hall
- A Clerical Error
- The Riviera Affair
- A Double Life

Available in book shops internationally in print, e-book and audio formats. Check the website for more information. www.jnewwrites.com

*

Meet Lilly Tweed – Former Agony Aunt, Purveyor of Fine Teas, Accidental Sleuth.

If you like twists and turns, red herrings galore and big crimes in small British towns, then you'll love the **Tea & Sympathy** Mystery series. Full of lively personalities, intelligent characters and excellent tea!

THE BOOKS:
- Tea & Sympathy
- A Deadly Solution
- Tiffin & Tragedy
- A Bitter Bouquet
- A Frosty Combination
- Steeped in Murder
- Storm in a Teacup
- High Tea Low Opinions
- Green with Envy

Available in book shops internationally in print and e-book formats. Check the website for more information. www.jnewwrites.com

About the Author

J. New is the author of **The Yellow Cottage Vintage Mysteries**, traditional English whodunits with a twist, set in the 1930s. Known for their clever humor as well as the interesting slant on the traditional whodunit.

She also writes the **Finch & Fischer** and the **Tea & Sympathy** mysteries, both contemporary cozy crime series.

Jacquie was born in West Yorkshire, England. She studied art and design and after qualifying began work as an interior designer, moving onto fine art restoration and animal portraiture before making the decision to pursue her lifelong ambition to write. She now writes full time and lives with her partner of twenty-four years, along with an assortment of stray cats and dogs they have rescued.

Printed in Great Britain
by Amazon